FEINTED LOVE

CRIMES OF THE HEART
BOOK 1

ELLE KEATON

DIRTY DOG PRESS

Prologue—Arnie

SEPTEMBER, *freshman year in college*

DUFF ABRUPTLY STOPS WALKING. I'm looking to the side checking addresses and not watching where I'm heading, so naturally, I slam into his back. My glasses end up hanging off one ear.

"Oof, jeez, Arnie," he complains, rubbing his arm as if I'd actually hurt him. I'm like one hundred and nineteen pounds fully dressed. I didn't make a dent.

"Are you sure about this?" I ask once I regain my balance and fix my glasses. We both gawk, eyes wide, at the *mansion* in front of us, its walls vibrating from the music blasting out of the open windows.

There's no doubt; we've definitely arrived at the right address.

The party house is four stories tall, white with four Grecian-style columns strung along the façade, making it look a little like the White House without the president.

The whole scene is very intimidating for a nerdy gay kid who's spent most of his life in a two-bedroom bungalow in the Greenwood neighborhood of Seattle. This part of Capitol Hill is rich. The houses are worth millions, and the residents mostly come from old Seattle money—or tech money. Kids who grow up here go to private schools and have memberships to swank clubs. A world apart from my life.

On the positive side, Capitol Hill also has Broadway and is one of the most diverse and accepting neighborhoods in the entire city. I looked it up once; gays have been living on Capitol Hill or downtown since at least the 1930s.

Duff shrugs. I'm jealous of my best friend's easy nonchalance. The way he's just Duff and no one questions him—no one's going to look twice at him and silently wonder if he was invited (spoiler alert: neither of us was). Duff belongs even though he's probably never met any of the other partygoers; I, on the other hand, am a permanent outsider.

As we watch, a few of the partiers spill out of the open front door and into the front yard. A park to some, a yard to others.

Duff cocks his head toward the open door. "Let's go."

I follow my best friend into the fray.

NO ONE PAYS any attention to our arrival. There are, at my estimation, at least fifty guys ranging in age from seventeen or eighteen to mid-twenties, all in various states of drunkenness, standing, sitting, leaning, taking up space on the first floor alone —and more outside in the backyard. Duff squeezes around a blond guy and a dark-haired guy who are lip-locked and grinding against each other, each with a red cup in one hand. How they can do that and not spill their drinks I have no idea.

I stop for a moment to watch, unable to decide if the display is hot or not.

The blond guy sticks his free hand down the back of the dark-haired guy's cargo shorts, pulling him even closer.

It's hot.

Duff leans back and taps me on the arm, dragging my attention back to him. "The bar's in the kitchen," he calls out over the din.

NO ONE CARES ABOUT two uninvited guests who are helping themselves to shots of tequila, a handful of pretzels, and more tequila. I figure Duff and I probably aren't the only uninvited guests, as there wasn't anyone watching the door.

We stick together for a while, hanging out in the living room, until Duff runs into someone he knows. Which I should've known would happen, but by now I'm feeling the effects of the tequila, so Duff wandering off is no big deal. And of course, when someone comes wandering around with a tray of Jell-O shooters, I have a couple of those too.

Squeezing the tiny paper cup, I tilt my head back, letting the cherry-flavored goo slide down my throat, and wrinkle my nose at the medicinal flavor. When the last drop is gone, I toss the cup onto the nearest surface and look around me, maybe a tad wobbly but at least not stiff with anxiety. Letting my gaze wander around the room, I wonder about the guys I see and make up little stories about them. There are a few girls present, but not many. "Get Lucky" by Daft Punk starts playing, and a few more partygoers head out to the makeshift dance floor.

The fact that this house is big enough to have a dance floor boggles my mind.

The two guys who were lip-locked when Duff and I arrived have moved into the living room. They're holding hands—just barely, fingers entwined—and I experience a stab of jealousy. That's what I want, someone to hold hands with and be myself with.

It's at that moment I notice *him,* standing on the other side of the room talking with another guy, his hands moving wildly as he tells his friend about something. It could have been the 1883 eruption of Krakatoa—I don't know or care, I just know I *need* to be closer to this stranger. I want to hear his voice; I want to know what color his eyes are and if he smells good. It may seem a bit weird to some people, but how someone smells can be a huge turn-on for me.

Teleporting across the room—that's what happens when you drink tequila—is the only explanation for suddenly being right next to *him.*

"Hey," I say.

That greeting comes out way smoother than I normally sound. I can totally do this.

The pretty blond guy *he* was talking to smirks at me before sauntering off, bumping *his* shoulder as he departs. making his way through the crowd, around the first couple I noticed, and out to the kitchen.

"Hey, yourself," Tall, dark, and handsome replies

He's tall—taller than me, anyway, with dark hair that has a slight curl to it. His eyes are an undefinable shade of green—or that's the tequila again, and I just can't find the right word. Greenish-blue. Blue. They're blue.

He smiles at me.

We're sitting on one of the couches, *together.* Somehow, I'm clutching a bottle of water. I lift it to my lips and guzzle what's left, knowing I have to be dehydrated. Some of the effects of the tequila have faded by now. I recall learning *his* name is Tobias, and this party is in his house. Tobias's parents and younger sister are off traveling, or something—maybe together, maybe not; I missed that detail, and I don't care as long as they aren't here.

"I'd like to travel someday," I say in response to the question he's asked, "but I have to pay for college first. And, to be honest, traveling alone scares me."

"Why you would travel alone? Wait—first, where does your dream trip take you?"

It's silly, at least it feels that way to me, but I've always wanted to visit Australia. I feel a spiritual connection with the country—even if it is almost eight thousand miles away. But since I've never left the West Coast, I can't imagine traveling to Australia anytime soon. It's a very long way from home.

"Australia."

"Why Australia?" Tobias asks.

I lift one hand to point at an area on my forearm where the skin is darker than the rest of me and shaped almost exactly like Australia.

Tobias looks at it. "It could be a kidney bean," he remarks.

"It's totally not a kidney bean! See the divot off the top?" I trace the top of my birthmark with my index finger. "It's definitely Australia."

"Hmm." Tobias raises a skeptical eyebrow.

I am suddenly and irrevocably distracted by Tobias's lips, my response lost somewhere in my addled brain. His mouth looks soft and... plush, and I want to find out for myself. I want to press my lips against those of the man I've just met who seems to be looking back at me the same way. I'm pretty sure he is, anyway.

The tip of Tobias's tongue appears, sweeping across his lower lip. Probably without the encouragement of Mr. Cuervo I wouldn't be as bold as I am in that moment, but I act on it—I lean toward him. Tobias meets me halfway. Our lips meet, and I am lost. The empty water bottle falls from my grip onto the cushion beside us. I clutch at Tobias's shoulders and open my mouth to taste him better. So he can taste me. I should be embarrassed about my reaction, about my erection, which is painful and stuck in the crease of my leg. My state will be obvious when I stand up.

But all I want is to feel more, more of Tobias. I want to know what his skin feels like. I want... more.

"Get a room," someone taunts.

Tobias breaks our kiss; his lips are swollen, and he looks as dazed as I feel. He peers back at me, his gaze full of promise. "You wanna go upstairs?"

Yes. Yes, yes, yes, yes.

Hell, yes.

ONE

Chapter One—Arnie

AUGUST, *seven years later*

I BLINK. What just happened?

One minute I'm innocently standing in front of Tougo Coffee minding my own fucking business, the sun in my eyes, an iced triple Americano in one hand, thinking about crossing the street so I can sit on one of the benches in Yesler Terrace Park to gather my thoughts and enjoy my coffee before a job interview.

The next, I'm wearing my coffee drink—as if an Americano is the newest fashion statement. I'm hip like that, always up with what's trending. It's the newest thing when interviewing: show up wearing clothes that look like they were pulled out of a trash can or I had a violent encounter with the milkman.

"What the hell?" I say—to no one, because the guy who tried to flatten me is about half a block away now. He glances over his shoulder. I catch his eye, but he doesn't stop walking. He doesn't even apologize!

"This is what's wrong with the world today!" I yell after him, "People like you, who think they can just, just... run into someone and get away with it!"

I stare at his back, but he doesn't turn around. Instead he disappears around the corner and is gone like nothing ever happened. My clothes are definitely ruined, or at the very least I need to throw them in the wash before wearing them again—so, maybe not ruined, but still!

Something about the guy niggles at me. His eyes. His hair, *something*, but I can't put my finger on it. With a sigh, I toss my sad, empty to-go cup in the trash bin and begin to make my way back down Yesler to my apartment in Leschi. It's a long walk in the warm weather, but it gives me time to calm down. I'm about ready to forgive the guy. I probably wouldn't have been happy working as a receptionist for a chiropractor; I'd applied on a whim. The incident was some sort of cosmic intervention, right?

That's when it hits me. I know that guy. Like, *know*, know him. And, now? Now, I'm really mad.

"TOBIAS BARRINGTON IS AN ENTITLED JERKFACE, and on top of that, he stole my virginity," I announce.

The only person who can hear me is my roommate, Duff, who is less sympathetic than I expect him to be.

"One, you gave it to him willingly, it was a consensual act, and two, you aren't getting it back. That was, like... years ago?" Duff mutters, only half paying attention to me as he scrolls through Snapchat on his phone while lying on our dusty floor.

"Maybe. Whatever, he set me on my life of dissolution and, you know... stuff."

"It was, quite literally, seven years ago."

"Yeah, and I've been stewing about it for seven years. I should've saved my V-card for Mike Riley or Seamus Twitch. What's that saying about giving away the milk for free?"

Duff sputters, trying to suppress laughter, I am sure.

"You're just pissed because Tobias Barrington has more money than god, and you're a barista at the Buzz."

Duff isn't wrong. The gap between Tobias's life and mine is about as big as the Grand Canyon. And seeing him brought all my old resentments to the surface. I'm fully aware they're petty —a person can't help who they're born to—but...Tobias Barrington, he was my first, and I've never been able to get him out of my mind. Amazing, considering the amount of alcohol Duff and I managed to swill before everybody got kicked out.

"Still, you want to know what happened today? Don't even try to guess." I stop him with a raised palm. "You won't believe it —I was innocently *minding my own freaking business*, about to head to an interview, and *wham*, this guy slams right into me. My very necessary sixteen-ounce triple Americano went flying and ended up all over me!"

"And," I add like I'm telling a ghost story to eight-year-olds at camp, "you know who it was? Who the cause of my doom was?"

"I can hazard a guess," Duff says, still looking at his phone and not displaying nearly enough sympathy for my plight.

"Tobias Barrington," I say triumphantly.

"Pretty surprising you recognized him, really, since he was probably wearing clothes."

"Duff! He didn't even apologize! He looked at me like I was a bug he'd squashed and practically ran in the other direction."

"Huh. And I'm sure you were calm, cool, and collected about it. *Not*. It was an accident, Arnie, and maybe he didn't recognize you. That party was a long time ago."

In reality, I hadn't stewed about the party that much. I don't think about it *every* day. Over the years, the *Tobias Barrington Incident* has declined in importance in relation to other disappointing life events. Like not getting into the college of my choice, my dad turning out to be a complete asshole, and not getting the job I wanted after my mediocre college career.

"Who the fuck has a name like Seamus Twitch, anyway?" Duff belatedly demands. "You made the name up, admit it."

I roll over on the ancient futon cushion to glare at my best friend, and something pokes me in the hip. "I couldn't make up a name like that."

I'd totally made it up.

Duff sighs and flops onto his back. Now he's attempting inexplicable leg stretches, making dust angels on the floor. Various joints pop, and I wonder how long it will be before he pulls something important and needs me to get him an ice pack and an ibuprofen. I make a bet with myself that it will be within half an hour.

"You taking yoga classes again?" I ask. I think I remember Duff having sworn off yoga after a particularly unpleasant hot yoga experience.

I wonder about Tobias Barrington. Does he do yoga? Maybe it's something I should consider. A chance meeting in a yoga class; there are worse places to accidentally run into someone. Tobias would probably look sexy in stretchy yoga pants. The fact that I am contemplating a fake-chance meeting via fake yoga should have me worried about my own mental health. That kind of exercise is for people like Duff. The Fergusons are short, skinny, nearsighted and not pliable at all. And I can't think about him being sexy when he was a dick.

"Um, maybe?" Duff replies.

"Is the instructor hot?" I ask.

"Maybe." Duff sounds a tad defensive.

The instructor is totally hot; there's no other reason for Duff to drag himself out of bed at six every morning for the past week.

"If you hurt yourself, I'm not covering your shift."

I totally would, though. One of us has to make enough to pay the rent. I refuse to ask my mom for help. Between modeling jobs, Duff fills in at the Buzz, but even Gale's decent wages (for a coffee shop) aren't quite enough. Hence, me making feeble attempts to change jobs.

Watching my roommate try to turn himself into a pretzel is almost painful. Instead, I stare up at the ceiling, watching as the cobwebs hanging in the corners of the room move sluggishly.

"I'm not going to hurt myself. Yoga is helping me open my chakras and stuff," Duff retorts.

Our "living room" is quiet for a moment, the only sounds the rustle of Duff about to hurt himself and the near-death whine of the desk fan we've jammed into the window in an attempt to entice a breeze into our tiny studio. Four hundred and fifty square feet seemed a lot bigger when there wasn't any furniture taking up space.

"He needs a lesson. He owes me."

I'm back to thinking about Tobias Barrington, who, I have concluded, needs a lesson in what it's like to *not* get what you want all the time.

"I think," Duff huffs out between stretches, "If he pays you for it, it's called prostitution."

"I mean, he owes me something. When our relationship is equalized, then..." My plan has kind of a hazy quality about it.

"Um, you didn't have a relationship then, and you don't have one now," Duff helpfully points out. "Tobias Barrington took you upstairs—I was at the same party, remember? You begged him, he took you upstairs and, I quote, 'fucked your brains out,' and you haven't spoken to him since."

I release a gusty sigh. "I didn't beg. I'm pretty sure *he* invited *me* upstairs. You're missing the point."

"I don't think there is a point."

Shifting positions on the couch, trying to find the breeze, I say, "There is a point, just like you and your chakras—which must be pretty blocked up, because you snore. Tobias took something that didn't belong to him, and after ignoring me for years has the gall to knock into me and spill my coffee." At this point I'm almost more upset about the coffee than the other thing.

I'm perfectly aware Tobias didn't take anything from me at the party that I wasn't willing to give. But I'm pissed off that he has the world at his feet, while I'm... at the feet of the world. Ugh, terrible metaphor. It sounds like I'm giving the world a blow job.

"I'm not explaining things right. Tobias is this rich guy. He can have anything he wants, right? Somebody needs to teach him a thing or two. I think it's going to be me."

Did he even know your name?" Duff wheezes out. "Was your life on track freshman year? Mine sure wasn't. And if you want him to pay for your clothes, which are all already covered with coffee stains, why don't you ask him?"

"Again, not the point. Points."

More wheezing from Duff. Something pops, and he groans and collapses facedown in a heap. I hate to think "I told you so," but I do. Only I think it in my head, not out loud.

"I'm going to need your help with this, with my Tobias Barrington project. Do you need an Advil?"

While I've been lying here, I've come up with a half-thought-out plan I think is pretty good. Okay, maybe it's more like a quarter thought out. I'll flesh it out further as time goes on. And, as Duff is my best friend, he's practically morally obligated to help me.

Operation: Teach Tobias Barrington a Lesson has a nice ring to it.

I mean, he didn't even apologize after running into me. I was left standing on the street with coffee dripping down my front and an interview I was definitely not making it to. Who does he think he is, anyway? An entitled jerkface is who he is.

"Maybe just frozen peas. There's a bag in the freezer," Duff replies.

Likely the only things Tobias Barrington cares about are money and his social standing among the other Rich Gay Boys of Seattle, as I think of them. The boys who grew up attending private schools and spending their summers at Madison or Madrona Beach oiling their chests or slumming on fifty-foot sailboats out on the sparkling blue waters of Lake Washington. Not that I'm jealous.

A good number of gay boys slum in the Leschi neighborhood where Duff and I work and live these days. We moved here my senior year in college. At the time, the makeup of the neighborhood didn't occur to me; I just wanted my own place. The area has a significant population of LGBTQ people, as well as being old money. Consequently, I see groups of rich gay boys almost every day over the summer as, two by two, they parade into the coffee shop, order their annoying special-order coffees, and leave, zipping off in overpriced sports cars to wherever they spend the day. To be fair, the straights act the same way, but I don't envy them.

Maybe a little.

"He came in to work last week," I say.

"Mmm," is Duff's response.

"He's been in a few times, actually."

"Arnie, should I be worried about what's going on inside your head?"

"If I get you a bag of peas, will you help me?"

Duff isn't moaning in agony or anything, but he's also lying very still. He slowly turns to face me. "Seriously, Arnie?"

"Duff, you're my best friend. You're the only person I can ask."

"Please bring me the peas."

Noticing he hasn't agreed to anything, I heave myself off the futon, step over Duff's prone form, and take another four steps to reach our kitchenette. When I open the freezer door, cold air rushes out, cooling my skin; I stand there for a minute with the door open, letting icy air work its magic.

"Are you going to stand there all day, or are you going to bring me peas?" Duff asks, his voice pained.

Rolling my eyes, I reach into the small freezer to grab the peas. They're hidden behind a carton of ice cream that seems awfully light, considering I only bought it a few days ago. I push the carton aside and grab the bag of veggies.

"Did you eat all my ice cream?" I ask in a slightly accusing tone.

"No."

"Did you eat *most* of my ice cream? Jeez, Duff."

The frozen peas are a solid block. They've been defrosted, frozen, and defrosted again more than once, and now they're stuck to the bottom of the freezer. Duff doesn't answer my question about the ice cream, but who else would've eaten it? A thought strikes me as I tug at the peas.

"Did you have someone over while I was at work?"

"Aargh, please, can I have the peas? Yes, I had someone over."

"You had someone over, ate my ice cream, and didn't tell me about it?"

"Arnie, I'm going to kill you in your sleep, and then you'll never get your revenge on what's-his-name."

"Tobias Barrington. And it's not revenge, it's a lesson." I

swing around to stare at Duff again. The bag of peas pops off from where it was stuck to the bottom of the freezer, I nearly lose my balance, and a few peas escape the bag to roll across the slightly sloped kitchen floor and under the refrigerator. Oh well. "So you're going to help me?"

"Fine, I'll help you with this ridiculous plan." Duff's voice is muffled, but I hear the words loud and clear.

Kneeling down next to my friend, I place the icy bag on Duff's lower back. "Awesome. You are the best."

He mutters something else into the crook of his elbow. I don't quite catch it; all I hear is "You think..." but I don't ask him to repeat himself. I probably don't want to hear it. All that matters is, he's agreed to help me.

TWO

Chapter Two—Tobias

"HE'S SO..."

"What, Charley? He's so *what?*"

"Rough around the edges."

I'm certain Charley had planned on saying "geeky" or something like that but changed his mind at the last second. I worry about my best friend. He used to be...happier, but in the past year he's become jaded and cynical.

"You don't need my help. If you want to talk to him, talk to him," Charley says helpfully.

"Charley, I need you to help me break the ice. I'll just freeze up and act like a jerk. And I might have run into him. Like, literally run into him."

Charley stares at me. "What happened?"

I cringe at the memory. "I was a bit late meeting a potential investor and not watching where I was going, and the next thing I knew coffee was flying. I was so embarrassed—and late—that I couldn't stop. I'm sure he thinks I did it on purpose or something."

"Okay... and you want me along, why, again?"

"I guess just... moral support. I know he works tomorrow tonight—" I feel my cheeks heat.

"You have his schedule memorized?" Charley asks in astonishment, his signature wicked grin spreading across his face.

"Kinda, I guess. I didn't mean to."

"And *he's* the guy you want my professional help with." Charley shakes his head at the thought, his longish blond hair swinging away from where he'd tucked it behind one ear. We've met up after work at a café he likes. The Sweetwater Cantina has a view of Lake Union from the patio, and the tequila selection is incredible.

I sip a shot of high-end tequila and wait, watching the sailboats tuck in against the wind. I know he'll help me, be my wingman, but he's going to bitch about it every step of the way. When I'd mentioned Arnie to Charlie, he'd immediately known who I meant. Funny that. I hadn't known Arnie worked at a coffee shop only a few miles from home until recently. And now I'd knocked coffee all over him. Way to go.

"I was thinking we'd go in together around seven and get something to drink, and you could strike up a conversation with him." Because, yes, I am a complete coward, and the glowers I've been on the receiving end of... Well, I probably need my head examined if I'm considering asking him on a date after exploding his coffee and leaving the scene of the crime, but no one ever said I was a genius.

"Tobes." Charley glowers. "If you want to ask him out, you're the one who needs to be striking up a conversation with him."

"I can't. I'm sure he hates me," I whisper.

Charley's eyebrows draw together. "Hates you? For spilling

his coffee?" He utters the words as if it's impossible that someone could hate me. "That's ridiculous. But say he does—which, if so, why would you want to ask him out—why do you think he hates you?"

"Aside from the coffee thing? Remember that party? The one you talked me into having while my dad was on a business trip, and the entire gay population of Seattle showed up?"

"That was an awesome party," Charley says nostalgically. "Those were the days."

"Until the police arrived." And even before that, I'd been worried and nervous about all the people there. But once the alcohol kicked in, it hadn't seemed all that bad—and my anxiety had lessened enough that I'd propositioned an adorable, sexy guy I'd never met before. "He was the guy."

"The guy?"

"*The guy*. Do I have to be any more specific?" Charley knows I'm not the kind of person who randomly hooks up with strangers. It had only been the one time. I've had plenty of boyfriends, but only once have I hooked up with someone I didn't know.

"The guy you took upstairs? Are you sure?" Charley asks, having heard my story about *the guy* a million times.

I nod. "I'm sure. Pretty sure. I was drunk that night, but I remember him. He had, has, this birthmark shaped like Australia on his arm, and I saw it when he was wearing a short-sleeve shirt at work."

"Let me just get this straight—excuse me, gay—so I am fully understanding everything here. You want me, Charley Hunter the third, to accompany you to a coffee shop so you can check out some random guy you messed around with a million years ago."

"If he was random, I wouldn't remember him!" I protest.

I've always felt bad about how the party ended. Arnie

Ferguson (I only learned his full name recently) and I absolutely didn't run in the same social circles. I'd given up on reconnecting with him ages ago, mostly forgetting about the whole thing... until a month ago when I'd stopped at the Buzz in the late afternoon, and there Arnie was in living color, my mystery man. In that moment I knew what it felt like to be struck by a bolt of lightning out of the clear blue sky. And I followed that up by knocking coffee all over him, which was not so much lightning as an earthquake. I can only hope he didn't recognize me. I wanted to die of embarrassment, and I couldn't stick around. The client had a plane to catch.

"What am I supposed to do? Charley asks with an air of resignation.

"I told you, he acts like he hates me. Except..." I recall that first time I walked into the coffee shop—one I didn't normally go to. It was about five in the evening, and the Seattle sun was nowhere near setting yet—it was a liquid heat blazing down on the city, and I was sweltering in the suit I'm forced to wear to work. Arnie (a convenient tag with his name on it was clipped to his apron) was behind the counter, wiping down the gleaming espresso machine. But I could've sworn when he looked up to see me approaching the bar, he'd smiled—a real smile that reached his hazel-green eyes behind the black rimmed glasses he wore. For me, time fell away. I was seeing Arnie for the first time again, and I liked what I saw.

"Heya, you look like you need something to pick you up. You've come to the right place. Coffee, tea..." Arnie'd called out, flapping his hands in the air, leaving the "me" unsaid, but I'd heard it.

Arnie was, hands down, the worst flirter I had ever met, but it was cute and sweet and surprisingly honest. And I liked it.

While I was waiting for my drink, I spotted the birthmark on his arm. Recognition made my stomach twist. I'd been almost sure it was him already, but... it had been a long time. This confirmed it, though: he had to be *the guy* from the party.

I'd been trying to come up with a casual way of mentioning it, working up to ask if he remembered me, but when I offered Arnie my debit card, he took a good look at me and turned from cute and flirty to stone cold, and since then, *nothing* I say has changed his reaction, no matter how many times I stop and get coffees I don't need. I don't even really like coffee that much, but I've had plenty in the past few weeks. Up until I bulldozed him anyway.

I've stopped by the Buzz so many times I know Arnie's schedule. I want to experience the warmth of his brilliant smile again, and regardless of the ice-cold shoulder, something keeps me returning for coffee and chilly glares. I am, obviously, a sucker for punishment. But more than once I've been sure I caught him watching me when he thought I wasn't looking, and his expression hadn't been cold at all. It had been wishful, or even longing.

What if I'm right? What if he does remember me, and he's too shy to say anything or thinks I don't remember him?

"Except what?" Charley demands, interrupting my thoughts.

"Except I could be wrong. And I just, you know, want you to pretend we're hanging out."

Charley's eyes widen, and he raises both eyebrows. "What do you mean, pretend? We hang out all the time."

I roll my eyes. "I mean *hanging out*. Like dating hanging out or something." I have another sip of tequila, enjoying the complicated and bitter flavor on my tongue.

Charley asks, "If he's giving you the cold shoulder, why bother? And you're like a brother to me. I'm not convinced we'll be able to pull it off."

Why bother is a question I keep asking myself but don't have the answer to.

"Please?" I bat my eyelashes.

This time Charley rolls his eyes as he shakes his head.

"All right, but..." He's tapping his lip. "I'm thinking this could go sideways. And no weird love triangles. That's not my thing."

Heat rises in my cheeks, and I silently curse my pale skin. "There's not going to be any weird love triangles. He'll probably keep ignoring me, and I'll quit getting coffee there."

But I hope not. I'm hoping Arnie will come around. Maybe Charley's acerbic wit will get a response out of him. I don't know, but I don't have another idea. Other than suddenly developing the balls to ask him why he doesn't like me, which isn't going to happen. I mean, I should apologize to him about the coffee thing, but he doesn't seem to want to hear it. "Hey, sorry about ruining your day a while back, do you think you might want to go on a date?" Nah.

"Seriously, why don't you just ask him out?" Charley asks as if he's reading my mind.

Instead of answering, I finish my shot, staring out at the lake again. Charley is right, asking Arnie out directly would be the simple solution... but I'm afraid the answer would be no, and I don't want it to be.

I've thought about that party on and off over the years. Since then I've been to dozens of parties—but occasionally a memory from that night will pop up, much like the Memories on Facebook or something, reminding me how magical my experience with Arnie was that evening and how empty I felt when he disappeared. Charley teased me for ages about Arnie being my Cinderfella, and I was fine with that—but I would've at least liked a glass slipper to track him down with.

And now that I've found him, he isn't making things easy for me.

THREE

Chapter Three—Arnie

OVER THE NEXT FEW DAYS, I can't stop thinking about my idea. It's as if now that I've come up with the concept of teaching Tobias a lesson, I'm possessed by it. I want to get started immediately; I've convinced myself that once things are evened out between us, my life will improve. How could it not?

I am likely blowing smoke up my own butt, but if it gets me out of food-service hell, I'm willing to try. I just need Tobias to stop by my work again. Next time I'm going to make myself smile at him.

I actually *want* to smile at him. When he comes into the coffee shop, which was every couple of days until he mowed me over and left me looking like a fool, I want to throw myself at him like one of those stupid moths that fly around, only to zap themselves out of existence when they come too close to electric bug killers. I snort, imagining Tobias Barrington as a gigantic bug killer.

Evenings are my favorite shift at the Buzz. I usually request them. Instead of impatient customers glaring at me because they're late for work—it isn't my fault they didn't get up on time, is it? It isn't my problem they had to look for parking or have a cranky kid in tow. At night, instead, I usually have people who are pleasant and polite.

Most evenings the shop is populated by couples or folks I assume are self-employed, quietly working away on their laptops or chatting with friends. Gale Harkness, the owner, lets me play whatever music I like and trusts me enough to let me work on my own. I'm on an oldies kick these days, and this evening an '80s mix is playing overhead while I clean up the espresso machine and the rest of the workstation. I'm sanitizing the back counter when a voice from behind me interrupts my thoughts. I was focused on cleaning up and hadn't heard anyone come in.

"Can we order some coffees?"

My heart lurches in my chest, but I keep wiping down the counter. I recognize that voice, and I'm not going to hurry for it. I am not that desperate. Right?

"Darling, you need to be much more assertive," says another voice. This one is new to me.

With precision I set the cleaning materials aside and turn to see who I'm going to be killing with my laser glare. I have a feeling, the kind my mom would call a premonition, that I'm not going to like what, or who, I see.

Tobias Barrington is waiting on the other side of the counter, and another someone, the voice I hadn't recognized, waits along with him. They are both dressed to slum. Tobias is so obviously a rich boy it makes my teeth hurt, as is his friend. I hate that I recognize the emotion I'm feeling as jealousy. My unfashionable glasses slide down my nose, I push them backup wishing I wasn't sweaty and hot.

Narrowing my eyes at the two of them, I ask coolly "What can I get you?"

"Tobias here has been regaling me with your coffee-making skills. I'll take a macchiato," says the stranger.

He turns to Tobias. "Tobes, what do you want? This is on me tonight." He turns back to me and asks, "Do I know you from somewhere?"

The jerk is about my height, with an artfully shaggy hair style that must've cost a pretty penny. His distressed T-shirt and pre-ripped jeans surely cost at least a month of my pay, possibly more. He doesn't hold a candle to the man standing next to him. Tobias Barrington makes my stomach do funny things. Funny things I'm trying to ignore.

Tobias scowls and pokes his friend with his elbow, presumably to shut him up.

"I doubt it," I respond in my chilliest tone.

Somehow the remark had sounded a lot more cutting inside my head.

I know I'm being rude, but Tobias's friend is bringing out my worst behavior. I can't help it if I'm a tad below average height while Tobias cornered the market on tall, dark, and handsome and his friend looks like he escaped from one of Duff's photo shoots.

"Sorry about Charley," Tobias says, although he doesn't sound sorry enough. "Can I have a double cappuccino to go?"

"Change mine to a cappuccino, and extra-stiff foam on mine," says the friend. waggling his eyebrows.

Gah, whoever he is, I hate him.

"Charley, do you think you can behave until we're back outside?"

Charley sighs dramatically. "I suppose, but you take all the fun out of everything."

Tobias and I both glare at Charley. I briefly imagine

Charley's faux-ripped clothing disintegrating off of his body, leaving him naked and exposed, in public. But then I realize this Charley person is no doubt an exhibitionist; being bare assed in front of hundreds of people wouldn't bother him. And he would likely be hot.

A tragedy is what Charley is. I should feel sorry for him. Likely he is dead and empty inside.

"Two cappuccinos, coming up." I turn my attention back to the espresso machine.

I promise myself I won't let Charley provoke me any further.

I immediately break the promise by reminding myself how Tobias, the jerkface, made no indication he recognized me and still hasn't bothered to apologize for trying to kill me the other day. He offers me a distracted "Thank you" and turns back to his friend, or date, or whatever he is.

Of course, a small, judgmental voice only I can hear whispers, "It's not as if *you've* said anything."

Like every other time I've served Tobias at the coffee shop in the past month or so, there's not a single sign from him that he remembers me. I wonder if Duff is right, Tobias doesn't recognize me, but frankly I just don't think that's possible. I fume quietly while pouring milk into the stainless steel pitcher. Tobias Barrington is the most arrogant person I've ever had the misfortune to meet.

Except for his friend, who is somehow even more full of himself. Go figure.

Twisting the knob on the steam wand, I heat the milk until it screams, a high-pitched whine meaning it's well beyond drinking temperature. I spoon the foam over the waiting espresso and shove the two go-cups across the counter.

"Enjoy your coffee," I say with a smile that feels too tight on my face. Jerks.

Tobias opens his mouth as if he's about to reply. I accidentally catch his friend's eye. He's amused, and it pisses me off, so I turn around and return to cleaning up the coffee station.

When I turn back around, they're gone, and I feel a stab of disappointment. Why did Tobias come in with that guy? Are they dating?

"Tainted Love" by Soft Cell comes over the speakers, and I find myself humming along. Maybe for the first time in my life, I actually listen to the lyrics, and damn if I don't agree with them. I mean, not that I love Tobias, or anything like that.

AFTER GETTING HOME THAT NIGHT, I take a cold shower, washing away the sweat and coffee grounds from my shift, and then lie in bed listening to Duff's quiet snores. Duff claims he doesn't snore, but I hear it every damn night he's at home. As I try to relax enough to fall asleep, I begin to flesh out my plot to teach Tobias a thing or two about life.

When I was eighteen, the world had been my oyster, a magical place where anything could happen. Since then the world has not lived up to my expectations, and the evening at Tobias's house seems to be the fated night where everything started to go wrong. It's a six-degrees-of-separation thing: every time I think about it, I find another reason why the party is at the root of all my current issues, why I am stuck in a dead-end job, not using my degree and barely making rent each month.

Crashing the party Duff had been told out about hadn't been difficult. By the time we arrived, guests had been spilling out from the house onto the porch and yard.

Inside had been an eighteen-year-old's wet dream. The house pulsed with pounding bass, the speakers pushed to their very limits by Lady Gaga belting out "Born This Way." Scantily clad men dancing alone and in groups in the enormous living room, free liquor, and no one who seemed to care Duff and I were uninvited. There was even a swimming pool in the backyard, completely ridiculous in the city—at least, until global warming really began to take effect.

A few hours later I was straddling Tobias Barrington's lap, in a passionate lip-lock. Duff had disappeared for a while too, but later he'd reappeared looking pleased and mussed—I'd actually forgotten about that part. What and who had Duff been up to that night?

Everything was incredible up until the moment I was lying in what I assumed was Tobias's bed, in a postcoital haze, planning the rest of our lives together, when he informed me it was time for me to go—I had to get up and get dressed, the police were coming and everybody had to leave. I mean, of course I know it was ridiculous to think Tobias and I were a thing. That he was my knight in shining armor.

Within minutes I'd found myself standing on Tobias's front lawn—only one sock on, my shirt inside out, my jeans barely over my hips, and my shoes in one hand—wondering what the hell had happened.

And things haven't gotten any better since then. All these years later, instead of changing the world I'm slinging coffee and living in a tiny studio I can barely afford. I feel like I'm permanently missing a sock and carrying my shoes around instead of wearing them.

DUFF WAKES me out of a sweaty dream as he tries to sneak out of the apartment just before six thirty the next morning. He tried to get dressed quietly, I'm sure, but he knocked something off his dresser.

"Yoga again?"

A wary look crosses Duff's face. "I talked to Jacob last night, and he thinks I should come to class, take it slow. Besides, I have a shoot coming up, and I always feel better when I've been stretching."

"Yeah, take it slow, I've heard *that* before. Maybe I should come with you to see just how hot this guy is."

Duff's eyes widen. I chuckle. He looks like a cartoon character when he does that. Although he has confirmed my suspicion that something is going on with the yoga guy.

"Nope, that's something I do not need you to do. Besides, you hate yoga."

"Maybe I need to try some new things, like quit hating on yoga. Tell you what, I'll stay away from your blessed yoga class if you really help me with my plan." I suspect Duff agreed so I'd bring him the frozen peas the other day, thinking I'd forget about it.

Duff squints at me, pulling on a pair of yoga pants and a tight T-shirt. "What plan are you talking about?"

I shake my head. "My plan to teach Tobias Barrington a little about life." I turn onto my side, propping myself up in one elbow. "He and his friend came in last night. Just another day of him rubbing everything in my face."

"Arnie?" Duff has a *tone* to his voice, one that tells me I'm not going to like what he has to say.

"What?"

"Does Barrington remember you? Has he ever said anything that indicates he knows who you are?"

Collapsing back onto the bed, I throw one arm over my eyes. "No. Maybe. I don't know. It doesn't matter if he remembers me. What matters is, the universe is out of whack."

"You're out of whack," mutters Duff. "If you promise to never set foot in my yoga class, I'll help you. What exactly is your plan?" I open one eye, and he shakes his head. "No, I don't want to hear it now; I'll talk to you about it later."

I recognize when Duff is trying to put me off, still hoping I'll change my mind or forget. But I'm not going to. "See, I've been thinking about it, and the only reason I'm at the Buzz is because of that party. Because of Tobias Barrington specifically."

"What? Have you lost your mind?" Duff stops moving toward the door and stares at me, his yoga mat tucked under one arm and a small towel tossed over his shoulder.

Groaning, I give up hiding and sit up. "Wait, hear me out. It's like this: we went to that party, and Tobias Barrington happened. Then you dragged me to Dick's."

Duff nods. "We were hungry and slightly drunk, and they're open until three a.m. Who doesn't want a Dick's burger?"

"Whatever, fast forward, and anyway, I haven't been able to eat there for years because I always think of him."

"Dick's—it makes sense. Seeing how much you hate dicks." Duff snickers at his little joke.

"Ha, ha, ha. Listen, it makes complete sense to me. See, Tobias—Dick's—the college exam—flubbing that interview with the city. It's all connected, don't you see?"

I wave my hands around, as if that will make everything understandable to Duff.

"How is that connected?" Duff is frowning as if I'm not making any sense—while if he would just listen to me, he would understand.

"I was *hungry*! And I can't eat there anymore! Dick's always reminds me of that stupid party, and then I get kind of sad, and..." I shrug.

"Dude." Duff shakes his head at me again. "I'm going to be late."

DUFF LEAVES, but I can't get back to sleep. I didn't sleep well, and now I'm going be tired all day, dammit. Tobias starred in my sweaty dreams. Apparently seeing him in real life last night at the coffee shop wasn't enough for my hyperactive brain.

"Arrrrggggghhhh."

That Charley friend of his bothers me so much. Plenty of my friends are snarky, but none of them are super judgmental. None of them call me "darling." None of them are complete assholes, which is more the point.

Heaving myself off the bed, I pad over to the closet Duff and I share. I open the door and stare at my clothes: folded, hanging, or stuffed where they fit into the small space. I try to look at the contents objectively. There are T-shirts and worn jeans (*real* worn jeans, not fake torn ones), the baggy sweaters I like during the chilly Seattle winters, six pairs of Doc Martens, and four pairs of Converse. One pair of uncomfortable oxfords stuffed in the back. I wore them once, a few years ago, when I interviewed for, and failed to land, the job I'd wanted after college graduation.

I had been hungry that day, and I'd messed the interview up.

On my way home, I'd been notified by email the company had already decided on another candidate. I'd been so upset by the news I'd gotten off the bus early and walked the rest of the way home, my shoes pinching and rubbing my heels.

Then I'd spotted the Help Wanted sign in the window of the Buzz. The rest, as they say, is history. Gale hired me on the spot and Duff not soon after.

But nothing about working at the Buzz employs my bachelor's degree in data science or my minor in Latin. As far as I can tell, the only thing my degree did was completely ruin my love of books and movies about demons and make me really good at obscure trivia. And research. I can research the hell out of anything.

The Latin used in movies is always, *always* terrible and so wrong. For crying out loud, Latin isn't that hard of a language—less than four thousand words. Surely a decent screenplay writer can come up with a well-written spell or summoning for demons. And why would demons speak Latin, anyway? I have questions no one can answer.

Too bad Duff isn't home; I could get him riled up about the demon thing too.

Regardless, it's clear, even to me, my wardrobe needs refreshing if I'm going to woo—*get even with*, I remind myself—Tobias Barrington and get a new job. I shove the closet door as far shut as it will go.

Maybe I should take my mom up on her offer to "buy you some respectable clothing." I generally hate respectable clothing. Suit porn is one thing—I can look at that all day long and all night too—but wearing a suit because you have to is another. Still, maybe my mom is on to something. If I'm going to infiltrate Tobias Barrington's clique and wreak havoc, I'm going to have to up my game.

FOUR

Chapter Four—Tobias

"SON, come to my study after dinner so we can have a brandy and a talk."

I mentally roll my eyes; am I actually living in Regency England and having a hallucination I live in the twenty-first century? Who, except my father, Andrew T. Barrington, has brandy in their study after dinner? I wish I'd taken Charley up on his offer to go sailing this evening, but my mother made me promise I'd be home tonight. I should've realized it was time for my annual review.

"Answer your father, dear," Olivia says.

I want to point out that it had been a statement and not a question. Instead I nod and close my lips around a forkful of salmon penne. The pasta is handmade by our household chef, the salmon flown in from Alaska just for us; it's dust in my mouth. My younger sister, Sarah-Michelle, gives me a covert sympathetic glance.

The dining room echoes with the quiet clinking of our

silverware against the Royal Doulton china used for our everyday meals. Harriet, the house manager (and more of a mother to me than my own), moves in and out of the room in that invisible way of hers, picking up dinner plates and returning with dessert—handmade sorbet tonight—which, of course, my mother politely refuses for both herself and Sarah-Michelle, even though she is the one who insists on full-course meals Monday through Saturday.

I already know exactly how the conversation in my father's study is going to go, because it's August, and for some reason August is the time of year Andrew rakes over my accomplishments as if he were giving me an annual review. *Son, you're getting an overall rating of two, for the second year in a row. That means no raise, of course, and that you still disappoint me on a regular basis.*

"TOBIAS, I have expectations for you as my son, and you have a responsibility to me as your father. The firm will be yours one day, and at this point I don't think you're competent to run it. If you were one of my staff, I'd give you three out of five. You're lackadaisical, unmotivated, and sloppy, and if you were anyone but my son, I would have fired you by now."

A three. I must've done something right.

I'm reasonably sure my father believes he's doing me a favor by being "brutally honest"—his words, and although I've heard them every August since I started college, they still sting.

I don't actually want to be a failure. I'm just not cut out to be a real estate agent or a property manager—I don't have the blood lust required for a career in the housing market. I hate working for the family business, and yet... here I am, still working for him and still living at home. And I have no one to blame but myself. Charley lives at home too, but his house is an actual mansion and he has a separate apartment.

I promised myself years ago not to leave Sarah-Michelle here on her own, so I went to the University of Washington and continued to live at home. As her big brother, six years older, I couldn't leave her to deal with Andrew and Olivia Barrington by herself. But in less than a year I'll finally come into the inheritance from my maternal grandmother, and Sarah-Michelle will be safely away at college—on the East Coast, or even abroad, if I have anything to do with her choice.

"Tobias!"

Crud, I'd tuned my father out—a habit I developed out of self-preservation, but usually I catch enough of what he's saying to be able to fake it. "Yes, Dad?"

"Did you hear what I said? Do I need to repeat myself?"

"No, Dad, I got it. I'm a disappointment, a failure, and I need to get my act together or you'll fire me." Please, *please*, fire me.

Andrew frowns from where he's seated behind his enormous mahogany desk, swirling brandy in a snifter before taking a sip. "No, Son, I won't fire you. Damn fine brandy."

Dammit.

"I have faith that you'll turn it around this year. I think what you need is an assistant. Someone who can take the inconsequential things off your hands so you can focus on finding properties and closing deals. I've got Carly working on that angle now."

I gape at him. An assistant is the last thing I need or want. I don't want my dad to hire someone to help me; I want to quit, I want to move out—I want something impossible. The last thing I need is an assistant following me around and reporting back to my dad that all I do is daydream eight hours a day.

· · ·

AS I LEAVE THE STUDY, I text Charley. DAD IS HIRING ME AN ASSISTANT.

NICE

NOT NICE

MAYBE IT WONT BE SO BAD, HOW BAD COULD IT BE?

I consider this for about thirty seconds. I know my father.

THERE'S NO WAY IT WONT BE BAD. I DON'T KNOW WHAT HIS ANGLE IS YET BUT...

Charley sends me a shrug emoticon.

I understand. He knows as well as I do that I'm quitting the business in April, so why am I complaining?

As I walk through the back of the house toward the stairs and the sanctuary of my room, I hear Olivia and Sarah-Michelle having a heated conversation in the kitchen. They stop talking as I enter the room. I can tell from the expression on Sarah-Michelle's face that Olivia was riding her about something. Sarah-Michelle isn't perfect. She's seventeen, after all.

"Hey, what's up?" I ask.

"Mom wants me to try out for cheer squad again. I don't want to try out for cheer. I've told her that hundreds of times," Sarah-Michelle says, her tone insinuating Olivia never listens—which she doesn't.

"Can't you just let it go, Olivia?" I say with resignation.

"They're holding special tryouts," Olivia replies, mulish.

I know as well as Sarah-Michelle does, the only reason Olivia wants her to try out for cheer is so Olivia can brag about her daughter being on the squad. Which would be fine, if it were something Sarah-Michelle wanted to do.

"I'm not going to try out." My sister crosses her arms across her chest. "If anything, I want to apply to the coding program the U is offering for high school senior girls. It's really competitive. If I got in, it would look amazing on my applications. I'm sorry if that's not cool enough for you, Mom."

Olivia starts in, "Nobody wants smart girls, Sarah-Michelle."

"Olivia." I cut her off, because this is going too far. "Has it ever worked out when Sarah-Michelle is forced into doing something she doesn't want to? Remember Girl Scouts? Remember tennis lessons?"

The kitchen is quiet for a moment while we all revisit our memories. Mine is when my sister had to be dragged off the tennis court. The other girl had accidentally hit her with her racket, and Sarah-Michelle—who already didn't want to be there—reacted... negatively. She could be on cheer if she wanted to. She's very coordinated.

"Fine," says Olivia. "No cheer, but we are going to fly to LA and tour Pomona College."

Sarah-Michelle sighs but nods. There are worse things than going on a college tour slash shopping spree.

FIVE

Chapter Five—Arnie

MY PHONE IS LYING on the floor next to my futon. Rolling over, I grab it, press Call, and then flop onto my back to stare at the ceiling while listening to the ring on the other end of the line.

"Heya, sweetie," my mom answers.

I wonder what she's doing this morning. When I was in high school, my dad ran off with his secretary as if he was living some sort of 1950s TV show, leaving Rita Ferguson to live her best life. She claims she's never been happier. I have a great relationship with my mom and a complicated one with my dad. I'd never ask him to help me buy clothing, and I'm pretty sure his new wife is a homophobic bitch. No hard proof, but I don't feel like I need to prove anything to know that the new Mrs. Ferguson is perfectly happy with me never visiting their house.

"Heya, Mom."

"Why are you calling me this early? Is everything okay?"

I hadn't thought about the time. I glance over at the digital clock on Duff's dresser and cringe.

"Sorry, Mom, I didn't think about what time it was. But I'm calling because I want to take you up on your offer to help me get some new clothes." I have to ask before I chicken out. As good a relationship as we have, having my mom help me buy clothes means she's going to want to help pick them out.

The connection is quiet for just a second, and I imagine her playing the request back in her head, making sure she's heard me correctly.

"Woot! Finally," she chortles. "Arnie's letting me buy him new clothes!"

I hear noises in the background, maybe a car horn.

"Where are you?" I ask.

"Having a latte."

I find myself agreeing to meet her in just a few hours at one of the downtown department stores. A chilly panic begins to set in, but it's too late to back out. My mom would show up at the apartment and drag me downtown if I tried to cancel our "date" now.

What am I doing? Revamping my wardrobe in order to teach Tobias a lesson? I'll really have to try harder to find a new job; that's the only answer. After clicking off, I shut my eyes, thinking about where I can feasibly apply. I do have skills and a degree I've never put to use. When I blink again, I'm groggy and disoriented. An hour has passed, and instead of coming up with a job plan I fell back to sleep.

I'm going to be late unless I get out of here in like thirty seconds. Taking one last look at the sad contents of the closet, I jam my glasses on my face, tug on a pair of probably clean Levi's, drag a sweatshirt over the T-shirt I find on the top of the laundry basket—it passes the sniff test—and then head out into the cool Seattle summer morning.

. . .

MY MOM IS WAITING for me at a table next to the outdoor espresso cart in front of the store. She looks happy, smiling and chatting with someone I can't see from my angle.

Calling out "Hi" as I approach, I brace myself for The Hug. Mom turns from her conversation, beaming at me. Even though she's my mom, I'm struck in that instant by how vibrant and beautiful she is. She seems to look younger now than she did when I was a teen. She is definitely happier.

"Arnie! I was just telling Sam here"—she indicates the person running the espresso cart, who's wearing a T-shirt that reads "Smile if you're gay"—"how you're a barista too!"

I try not to roll my eyes. Sam gives me a small smile, and I know, even worse than telling Sam I'm also a barista, she's been telling him I'm single and gay. She probably thinks two baristas together would be a perfect match. My mom wants me to have a boyfriend almost worse than I do.

"Heya, Mom."

She has always been my biggest supporter. When I was six, desperately wanting to be a garbage man, she told me I could do anything I put my mind to. Trash collection was quickly forgotten the summer I watched the Olympics... and the men's gymnastics competition. For years, Mom made sure I got to gymnastics on time, and when the coach informed me I wasn't talented enough to make the elite team, she consoled me.

As I close the distance between us, she stands from her seat to greet me with the expected huge, squishy mom hug. I actually feel my spine crack.

"Mom, it hasn't been that long since I saw you," I grumble over the top of her head. She's one of the few people in my life shorter than I am.

"It's been weeks! And you're going to let me buy you new

clothes; this is a dream come true." She squeezes me one more time before releasing me and stepping back. "Coffee, or should we just get to the good part?" She actually rubs her palms together like some sort of conspirator.

I smile at her. "Let's go inside."

IT PROVES impossible to keep my mom out of the dressing room. Brad, the metrosexual guy stationed in Men's Furnishings, thinks she's hilarious and lets her do whatever she wants, including waltz in and out of the changing area.

Because it's early on a Tuesday, there are very few other shoppers. Brad, egged on by my mom, keeps bringing me clothing until there are five suits and an unknown number of slacks, dress shirts, and "casual Friday" outfits strewn about the small room.

Seeing myself in a suit is weird. There's no other word for it: it's weird. I'm used to spending my days in ratty T-shirts and jeans. The suits make me look different. They make me look older and... sort of adult-like. I'm twisting around to make sure my ass also looks good, when my mom bursts in.

"Mom, one of these times I'm going to be naked."

She rolls her eyes. "Pssh, I've seen it all. You came—"

"No, no, no." I cut her words off. "I do not need a birth reenactment."

"Thirty-six hours of labor, and you were still born natural; I think I can talk about it all I want. But anyway, that suit is gorgeous. I love the way the gray highlights your eyes."

I'd believe her if she hadn't uttered the same words about every suit I've tried on so far. But I agree with her about this one. "Yeah, I like it."

"He's found one he likes, Brad!" she calls over her shoulder.

Before I know it, Brad is in the dressing room too, plucking and pinching and tugging everywhere, making sure the suit is a good fit.

"We'll need to have it altered in a few places. It's a little long in the legs." Brad has more clothing hanging over his forearm. "I found these too; I'll just hang them here for you to try."

I glare at him, and he leaves, but not before winking at me. My mother did not get the hint; she stays behind.

"I'm so excited for you, Arnie. Are you going to tell me what brought about this change of heart?"

Am I going to tell my mom that I want revenge on Tobias Barrington for stealing my virginity back when we were in high school? No. But the words that pop out of my mouth are potentially worse.

"I'm applying for jobs, and I have a few interviews I need to look good for."

She gasps. "A new job? No more coffee shop? Where? Are you going to try and get something in your field? Oh, honey, I am so proud of you."

I unbutton the suit pants; Mom does not take the hint.

"Um, yeah, it's time and all."

"Where have you applied?"

"If I tell you, will you let me change in peace?"

She laughs. "Yes, my dear son, I will. Now spill."

"Barrington Properties."

Again, it's the first thing that came to mind, and the worst. Somehow, during my planning and plotting, I'd forgotten a *very important detail*. I'd never told my mother about Tobias, and I normally tell her most everything.

"That jerk?" She frowns. "Why would you want to work for him?"

And she dislikes Tobias's father, Andrew—she knew him back when they were at the UW together, and since then Andrew Barrington has been one of the forces behind a lot of the gentrification of Seattle neighborhoods, including Greenwood.

She narrows her eyes at me thoughtfully. "On the other hand, this could work out perfectly." She actually cackles, which makes the little hairs on the back of my neck twitch.

I'm not exactly sure what would be perfect about it. "I'm applying other places too, Mom." I'll think of what the other places are soon.

She waves a hand dismissively. "You'll need to, of course, but we'll get you the job at Barrington, and then we'll have someone on the inside. I'm going to pick out a few power shirts." If anyone was wondering where I get my flair for the dramatic from, spoiler alert: It's my mother.

She disappears, and I'm left standing there with my pants unbuttoned, wondering if this current hell will be worth the possible outcome.

"DUDE, where the hell are you going to put all of that?"

Mom had dropped me and my bags stuffed full of new clothing off at the apartment—which meant me risking my very life in her car. I managed to convince her not to come upstairs with me. She's tiny but takes up a lot of emotional space, and I'm worn out from the morning of shopping.

"There're a couple of suits being altered too. And I don't know. I guess we're going to have to get a bigger apartment," I answer.

"We can't afford a bigger place."

"When I get a new job, we can."

"Since when are you getting a new job? Is that what all these clothes are about?"

"Kinda. They're part of my scheme to realign my life. Well,

to get something aligned anyway, and a new job is part of the plan. I'm going to apply at Barrington Properties."

"Yeah, I'm not convinced about this plan. Why do I have to help, again?" he asks.

I drop the bags onto my folded-up futon bed. "You agreed," I remind him. "You can't back out now. I actually went clothes shopping with my mom!"

Duff sighs but doesn't say anything.

"I need to do some reconnaissance, but I *think* I need you to do something about Tobias's friend Charley."

"Why?" Duff frowns. "And why are you using words like reconnaissance, anyway?"

I hated Charley on sight, but I don't think I should tell Duff that. Duff might figure out my dislike is about more than just getting even for the past. That *possibly* I'm jealous of him. To be honest, I don't think they're dating, but he pisses me off anyway.

"Reconnaissance is what you do when you're planning an op like this. And I need to focus on Tobias. I can't have that Charley dude around interfering with my plans." I wonder if they are dating, they don't seem like boyfriends to me. Or at least what I think boyfriends should act like.

If Tobias were with me, I'd want everyone to know we were together.

"God, you are weird. I should've listened to my instinct when we first met in eighth grade. What about my SUP instructor?" Duff whines. Yoga, stand-up paddleboarding, kayaking, rock climbing—what sport hasn't Duff tried out at least once? Especially if there's a hot instructor.

Now it's my turn to sigh. I narrow my eyes at him. "What about him? I haven't met this guy yet, have I? How serious is it? What happened to yoga guy?"

Duff is very good looking, taller than me (not difficult) with blond hair that more often than not is a tangle he pulls away from his face with a hairband. He and I have been best friends since middle school. We both figured out we were gay at the same age—but not gay for each other, thank god. Duff is a serial dater. He floats from one relationship to another, but he's currently, and amazingly, single—which means he's just hooking up with guys, not sleeping over. I think. When Duff dates, I get the apartment to myself, and when the breakup happens, Duff returns. Like now.

"Now is the perfect time, while you're not... doing your thing."

Duff squints at me. "Doing my thing?"

"You know, meeting a guy only to decide later he's an asshole, or clingy, or he messes with your spiritual center and come crawling back to your best friend. Who of course totally loves you." I add the last bit to take the sting out of my words.

While I talk, I begin pulling shirts and pants out of the bags and sorting them into tidy piles, deciding the best way to organize them in my part of the small space.

Without replying to me, Duff stalks into our tiny kitchen. I hear him turn on the faucet and pour himself a glass of water. I finish sorting my clothes, then open the closet door.

Eventually Duff says, "Fine. I said I'd help you, so I will. But I don't know Charley at all."

I feel a grin begin to crease my cheeks, which I suppress before turning to face Duff. "That's okay. I think Gale knows him; she knows everyone. I'll talk to her and get her to introduce you two, or something."

"Tell me the rest of this ridiculous plan." Duff sets the glass next to the sink and comes over to stare into the closet with me.

"I need you to figure out what this Charley guy is all about: is he friend or foe?"

Duff rolls his eyes. I want to warn him they might stay that way. "I still don't understand why it has to be me who runs interference with Charley," he grumbles.

"Because"—I sigh; Duff can be so oblivious sometimes—"while you're doing that, I'll make friends with Tobias." I add, "If I land a job at Barrington, it will be even easier. And, once I've lured him to me, I'll disappear into the ether. Teach him a thing or two."

"Since when are you applying at Barrington? And, as your friend, I'd like to point out that it's much easier to be straightforward and, you know, just make friends without all the high jinks. Also, this whole plan is ridiculous."

Ignoring Duff's common-sense response, I reach into the closet to grab a stack of T-shirts, the too-small suit, and the dress shirts dating back to my early teens and toss them onto the floor.

I stare at the pile. "These are going to have to go. I'm reinventing myself."

Duff is quiet for a moment. Then he says, "Arnie, you know you don't need to change yourself, right? I mean, if getting a new job is what you want to do—cool, go for it. But Tobias, he should like you for who you are inside. I know you have this idea you're not enough, that you're weird and quirky... and you are. Those things make you Arnie. Whoever you end up with should know the real Arnie Ferguson. Not some false Arnie you're inventing to get Tobias's attention."

I hate it when Duff gets all philosophical. And he's wrong. No one has ever wanted me for who I am (except my mom and Duff, and they don't count): school friends, ex-boyfriends, my own father didn't want me for who I am.

SIX

Chapter Six—Tobias

A FEW DAYS after my annual review, Charley and I meet after I get off work. I spend most days shadowing my dad and listening while he bosses his minions around. I'm supposed to be observing and using my dad as a model for when it's my turn to take over the company—gag. I hate it, hate it with a passion so passionate I have no words to describe how I feel about it. I think maybe it wouldn't bother me so much if he would just quit hovering and let me learn on my own.

My dad never listens to me when I try to tell him this. He ignores anything that doesn't directly involve Barrington Properties. Sarah-Michelle would be much better at my job than I am, but mentioning her as a possibility is forbidden. My dad has outdated social views, and one of them is that men do men's work (anything with money) and women do other things. So what if Sarah-Michelle is a National Merit Scholar? It infuriates me that our parents treat us, me and my sister, like dolls to be dressed up and taken out as they please.

"You'll be the one to take over the family business one day, Tobias. It will be your empire to run."

A fucking broken record.

What would happen if I told Andrew Barrington, that I, his son, am taking an online screenwriting class and hoping to get a master's degree in film? Originally, I'd wanted to major in English in college, but he insisted on finance and a business degree if he was going to be paying for my education.

"A humanities degree?" He'd laughed and whacked me repeatedly on the back as if I'd been choking on something. "Don't be ridiculous! An English degree won't pay out. Those guys waving signs on the corners all have English degrees. You will not be one of them."

I hated every second of my business classes, but at the time it seemed easier to agree to his terms. I'd hoped he would leave me alone once I complied, but no, two years after graduation I'm still required to follow him around and act like I care. Nothing I've ever said changed his mind.

Maybe my dad was right, and an English degree would've been useless, but it also would have been nice to find that out for myself. Why couldn't I have one of those rich dads who didn't care what his family did? Like Charley, who'd gotten a degree in art history and gone on to museum curatorship—until the big disaster, anyway.

OUR USUAL HAUNT is a funky old-time bar on Broadway called the De Luxe. The burgers are great and the atmosphere welcoming to people from all walks of life.

As usual, when the two of us come through the door, everyone's attention focuses on Charley, who shines like the first sunbeam entering a dusty room. I'm used to it, and I think the fact that I don't mind is one of the reasons Charley and I are friends. I hate being the center of attention. Also, the Charley factor is handy when I need a drink—like now—because the waiter stops by our table within minutes of our arrival.

"Moscow mule," Charley says.

"Make it two," I add. I want to make it a double, but I'll start slowly tonight.

"That kind of day?" Charley asks.

I nod. "Every time I bring up doing something different, Andrew keeps talking as if I haven't said anything at all."

"Have you tried quitting again?"

"Not since that one time," I mutter.

I'd told my dad I was quitting, maybe a year ago, and his face turned red so quickly I thought he might have been having a heart attack. The next several hours of lecture on how I owe everything to Barrington Properties, and to him, were torture—and then Olivia had gotten involved and there'd been tears, privately from me and publicly from my mother. In the end I'd let Andrew have his way, and I still am.

"We could empty our bank accounts and run away to LA," Charley offers.

Charley would, too, that's the kind of friend he is.

"I love Seattle," I say. "I don't want to move to LA, or anywhere else." I add pitifully, "You go ahead without me."

Charley shakes his head. "Nah, I'm a Seattle boy too."

And so is Simon Ellison, who broke Charley's heart. Secretly, I'm certain Charley is still hung up on Simon, but I never dare to say anything about it. Simon is a forbidden subject, even for me.

"Let's talk about something fun," Charley says. "Like how easy it is to rile up coffee boy."

I'm about to point out that Arnie Ferguson is not a boy when the waiter drops off our drinks, the copper mugs gleaming in the early evening light. He's cute enough—skinny jeans, a nose ring, and dark hair pulled back from his face—and all his attention is focused on Charley.

"Did you want to order anything to eat? Happy hour is on for another half hour."

I order a burger, while Charley orders a salmon Caesar salad made with kale. I make a gagging sound.

Charley raises an eyebrow. "So, coffee guy..."

"His name is Arnie."

"Coffee guy to me, until he decides to learn my name."

"I *like* him, Charley."

"You don't even know him."

"I know a little. He's maybe a year or so younger than me, he graduated from a high school in north Seattle, and he has a degree in data science." I can online stalk as well as anyone.

And, even though it was ages ago, I remember what it was like to be with Arnie, how good he felt in my arms, and how horribly disappointed I was when the police arrived and broke up the party. My one and only rebellious act; I'd been grounded for an entire year.

"First of all, I don't want to know how you found that out—but still, second of all, you don't really *know* him."

I sigh but nod, because it's true. "But I *want* to get to know him." How do I get to know someone who seems to hate me? And who my dad is certain to despise.

As if reading my mind, Charley says, "Your dad will hate him. I suppose there's not a better reason to date the guy."

Andrew will hate Arnie. And he won't be polite about it. If the two ever meet, my dad will take one look at Arnie and immediately know how much he makes, where he buys his clothing, how much he has in savings—and that information will leave Andrew cold. As he puts it, he doesn't mind much that I'm gay, but I should date in my socio-economic zone.

I glance across the table. Charley is watching me closely. I sigh again. "Maybe if I manage to date Arnie, my dad will get so angry he fires me and forgets I exist?" I hadn't considered that angle before. It was a possibility.

"There's always hope. Have you come up with a strategy?"

"Not anything more than to keep going into the Buzz when he's working until he gives me some sort of sign—or gets a restraining order."

"Hmm." Charley sips at his drink while he considers my problem.

While Charley plots, our food arrives. We eat silently, both lost in thought. This is one of the things I appreciate most about Charley: he never cares that I'm not super chatty and don't always have something to say. We're very opposite personalities, but we mesh. I only wish we were remotely attracted to each other; it would solve a lot of my troubles. My dad may not approve of Charley on a personal level, but his family has even more money than ours.

"Okay," Charley says. "I'll drop by the Buzz a couple more times with you, mostly so I can rile him up—it's fun." He laughs. "And then I think you need to fly on your own. See if you can catch him coming in for his shift, or even better, getting off work. Then just talk to him. Don't let yourself get in your own way."

"I'm really bad at talking," I remind him.

"But you're not," Charley says. "You just need to break the ice."

Somehow, I think Charley's idea of breaking the ice is different from mine.

SEVEN

Chapter Seven—Arnie

DURING MY SHIFT the next morning, I corner Gale in the break room the first chance I get. Hastily, I sketch out my Tobias plan. I figure the quicker I get the information out, the less foolish I'll sound.

Maybe.

"You're doing what now?" she asks, cocking her head at me. "Your virginity, where? Lesson teaching? What plan is this?"

I'm attempting to delicately share the tragic tale of my lost virginity with Gale and explain how I'm planning to even the scales of life, but halfway through my story she starts laughing so hard tears stream down her cheeks. As luck would have it, no one else comes back to the break room looking for either of us. I mean, honestly, it's beginning to sound more and more ridiculous, even to me—and I came up with the idea.

"I'm getting my V-card back. I mean, I'm redeeming my V-card, which will in turn get my life back on track. Ugh, look: Tobias Barrington is a rich, entitled jerk, and I want to teach him what it's like to *NOT* get everything you want. I want to take his silver spoon and... do something really bad with it." Wow, that sounds pathetic, and even I have to chuckle.

For some reason this makes Gale laugh even harder. She's bending over at the waist, supporting herself with the time clock while she howls, her laughter echoing off the walls of the small space. I stand there with my hands on my hips, a half grin on my face as I watch her, because yeah, it is a pretty silly idea. Eventually her shoulders stop shaking and she lets go of the time clock to stand up straight.

After wiping her eyes, she speaks. "I'm sorry. Look, Arnie, I don't think your V-card is your issue. It's not like you're going to get it back. It's not a bus pass. And I don't think you have a problem—you're doing fine. It takes some of us a little more time to find our footing than others. There is no guidebook to life, although one would be handy." She stares at me. I try to look, well, like myself. "But if you really want me to introduce Duff to Charley Hunter, I will. Charley's a little younger than me, but we know each other, and he owes me a favor. I'll take care of the introductions next week."

I don't want to ask what kind of favor Charley Hunter owes Gale, but my curiosity is piqued. "But—" I try to argue. Now that I have a plan (of sorts), I want to implement it immediately.

"Next week, grasshopper. If you want me to help you with this scheme, you're gonna need to let me plan my end of it the way I think it should go—and I do actually have a life of my own. Tell Duff he should probably clean up; Charley seems to like his boys all preppy and shit. Now, get to work. I'll catch up on the dishes in the back."

Out front, I tidy up behind the counter and then wipe down the tables, making sure we're ready for lunch. Summertime in Seattle means the shop is busy all day, unless it's raining. The beaches and piers along Lake Washington fill with Seattleites attempting to cool off—or just look cool. Duff calls them the spawners, although, as I've repeatedly pointed out to him, more than one pier juts out over the lake, and not all of them are populated with the spawning type.

"DUDE, it's time for you to punch out."

I look up from the dish I'm rinsing off. "Punch what?" I may not love this job, but I don't want to punch anyone.

My co-worker Eli rolls his eyes at me. "Punch out. Your shift is over."

I've been so lost in thought I didn't notice the time.

Once I clock out, I untie my apron and toss it in the staff laundry before heading out into the August sunshine—and slam directly into the object of my obsession.

Research. It's research.

"Whoa, in a hurry?"

Tobias's deep voice rolls through my body like thunder, stunning me; warm hands grab my biceps, keeping me from falling backward. I feel like how I imagine fish do when fishermen use illegal explosives for a better catch—floating around in the water, not knowing which way is up.

"Are you okay?"

I blink and snap out of my fugue. "Fine. Sorry, I was thinking." *About you*, but I manage to shut my lips against those words.

Tobias Barrington is so damn handsome. If I could've dreamed up a man just for myself, Tobias would've been my special order; he is everything I crave, and he has extra toppings. Thick black hair that curls up at the ends as it grows longer, pale skin—this close I can see a faded scar at one corner of his luscious lips. And blue eyes, the kind that are almost green but not quite, eyes I could lose myself in.

Tobias's eyebrows draw together. "Are you sure you're okay?"

I nod, stepping back and out of his grasp. "Yeah, sorry, I just got off work." I gesture behind myself. "I was in the pit today, uh, washing dishes; it was really hot in there." Anything to get Tobias to ignore my awkward daydreaming. Although telling him I've been washing dishes at my just-over-minimum-wage job doesn't make me feel much better.

"Oh, I bet, it's hot today." Tobias smiles.

If I'd thought I was in dangerous territory a minute ago, now my internal alarm bells are clanging so loudly I'm pretty sure I can actually hear them. Tobias's smile is brilliant.

"Can I buy you a drink? I bet you're dehydrated. And I kind of owe you one," he says quietly.

Tobias has a dimple in one cheek. Fuck.

"A drink?" I echo. What does he owe me a drink for?

Tobias's smile widens further. I don't know what to do. The dimple is distracting me.

"Yeeesss, a drink, a liquid, something to hydrate you." He chuckles. "The Madison Pub's patio is open. So is the Blue's. You could probably use a little time outdoors; you said it was hot in there today."

Someone bumps into me as they move around the two of us to enter the coffee shop. I have the dual realization that we're blocking the door and that no way should I have a drink with Tobias. Except I want to.

Why am I thinking about passing up this opportunity? I can have one drink. It's probably a really bad idea—I'm not prepared —but I'm going to do it anyway. After all, he said he owed it to me.

"Um, I have to get up early," I babble.

Really, Arnie? Get up early? This is why I hardly ever got

into trouble when I was a kid: I learned early on that I could not lie.

Tobias checks his watch, a silver Rolex with an indigo face. "It's only three thirty. But if you can't, that's okay. Maybe another time?"

Is it my imagination that Tobias seems disappointed?

"I, um, have an appointment," I fib. "I can't stay for long. And I stink," I blurt out. An appointment? All I could think of was an appointment? "An interview, I mean." I hope, anyway, someday to have an interview.

Tobias had started to turn away, but at my words he turns back. "We can sit on the patio, and you smell fine to me."

I look around for Charley Hunter. The last few times I've seen Tobias he's been with that absolute tool of a friend, or whatever he is.

"Where's your friend?" I ask. "The skinny blond with the terrible sense of humor?"

Tobias chuckles again. I nearly die. Still, I manage to scowl and narrow my eyes.

"I'll have a drink with you, but not if he's going to show up." I look around as if Charley might be hiding behind Tobias or maybe in the shrubbery.

"Charley has an event tonight. He's busy getting ready."

"Is he planning his own funeral? That's an event I'd attend."

"If you come have a drink with me, I'll tell you."

How could I resist?

We end up at the Blue; it's the closest of our choices and has two outdoor patios, one looking out over the lake and the marina, the other on the street side. It's a casual place, so the fact that I'm wearing a sweaty T-shirt and jeans doesn't bother anyone.

"Inside or patio?"

"By the water, please," Tobias tells the hostess.

There's one spot open, and we squeeze in on either side of a small table. I'm grateful for the umbrella keeping the sunshine off my head. A light breeze is blowing too. I hope it doesn't change directions. I'm sure I smell no matter what Tobias says.

"Can I bring you some drinks to start?" the hostess asks.

"I'll have a Johnny Utah."

"I'll have the same," Tobias says.

She heads off to place the order, leaving us alone.

"So," I begin.

"So, an interview?" Tobias parrots with a smile.

"You were going to tell me about Charley Hunter's funeral," I say to veer from the topic of a fictitious interview.

"Oh, right." Tobias's smile broadens. "He's been helping a friend plan a big cocktail party, and Charley needs to be there to make sure everything goes off without a hitch. He's kind of an event planner, but he also supplies social support."

Something about the way Tobias delivers the information seems off, but I don't care. I'm not here to learn more about Charley.

The waitress drops off our beers, and instead of saying anything, I snatch mine up, taking several deep gulps to quench my thirst and hide my nerves. It tastes incredible.

Tobias watches me before he too takes a long drink.

"Why did you ask me for a drink?" I blurt after I put my glass down.

I'm sure this time: Tobias blushes, and a sheepish expression crosses his face.

"You looked hot and thirsty. And, Arnie, I really need to apologize for knocking into you last week. I am so, so sorry. Do you need me to pay for cleaning or anything? There's no excuse, except that I was late and the client couldn't wait; I couldn't stay. I feel terrible about the whole thing."

Wow, way to punch a hole in my master plan—the man

apologized, and not only is he buying me a drink, he's offering to pay for my ratty clothes to be cleaned.

"I was thirsty. Thank you." I swallow the last of my beer. "Don't worry about my clothes. It's no big deal. And anyway, I wrangled up some new ones for my job search."

"Are you sure?"

I nod. "Yes, it's fine." I want to make him laugh. "Unless it wasn't an accident, and you were trying a new way to meet people."

He does laugh; it gives me a pleasant ache in the center of my chest.

"So, tell me about this new job."

Crap, I'm going to have to... what's it called when people make shit up on the spot? Improvise. "Interview. I probably won't get the job, so I'll still be at the Buzz."

"What are you looking for?" He honestly seems interested.

"I have a degree in data science and a minor in Latin—the Latin won't get me anywhere, but data studies is basically a lot like library science, and I can research the hell out of anything. I love research."

It belatedly occurs to me that Tobias usually shows up a bit later in the afternoon, and he isn't wearing his normal business suit. "Were you not working today?" I ask him.

"I played hooky today. My dad is pissed off about it, but I get vacation time just like the rest of the hacks. I know I'm awful, since it pays well and everything, but... I kind of hate my job."

"That sucks," I say, taking another sip of my beer before realizing it's empty. I watch him over the rim of my glass. His eyes seem sad now.

"Yeah, it's not what I really want to be doing."

"What do you want to do?"

Is it my imagination—did Tobias blush again? That must be

some sort of record. I didn't know anyone could blush more than me.

Tobias picks up one of the coasters sitting on the table and begins to fiddle with it.

He opens his mouth, shakes his head, then seems to change his mind before saying quietly, "I want to write movies —screenplays."

"Oh, yeah? Like *Terminator?*" I ask.

Tobias laughs, then, speaking a bit louder, says, "No, more like *Little Miss Sunshine* or *Napoleon Dynamite,* but also more serious stuff."

"How do you even write movies? And why do you want to? What got you started?" And now I want to bring up my theory about demons and Latin.

Tobias laughs again, his blue eyes meeting mine and making my heart do funny things.

"I guess I'm a movie nerd. I've always watched a lot of them." He shakes his head. "I'm not playing a poor-me card or anything, but my folks didn't pay much attention to me or my sister as kids—I had a lot of time on my hands."

Immediately I want to know more about what screenwriting actually is, how it's different from writing a novel or short story. How do you learn to do it? This is how my mind works: I love learning about obscure things other people might not know— and screenwriting fits right in. And, of course, the whole demon thing.

"Tell me all about it," I demand, leaning toward him. "Do you have things, movies, written already? Isn't Seattle kind of a bad place for movies? Don't you need to be in Hollywood?"

Tobias raises his sexy, sharp eyebrows at all my questions, but I can tell he's flattered I'm interested.

"Let's see, I'll try to answer in order. Um, I'm taking some online classes right now. I want to get a masters in screenwriting." He laughs a little bitterly. "Who knows if that will ever happen. I have some of my own ideas, but they're only six or seven sentences scribbled in a spiral notebook at this point. As far as LA goes, I'm not a fan. I've visited, and it's not my scene. I hope to be able to stay in Seattle, but I suppose I'd have to travel there often—if I am successful." He cocks his head. "Did I get everything?"

I nod. I want to know more, but it's clear I'm going to have to do some research on screenwriting to figure out the right questions to ask him. I have so many questions. And I bet he has a lot more than six or seven sentences written down.

I'm about to ask him where his ideas come from, but we're distracted by a little girl walking past our table leading a roly-poly chocolate lab puppy on a leash.

Once the puppy waggles on down the walkway, it's time for me to depart. I need to get home. Really look for a job. I've told so many people now, including Tobias, that I'm looking, I should probably actually do it.

"I should go," I say. "Thank you for the drink; I guess I really was thirsty." Smooth, Arnie, I mutter to myself, feeling awkward again.

Tobias pays for our beers, even though I try to pay for my own. "I invited you," he insists.

Together we exit the patio. I cross the boulevard and start walking toward my street just a block away, and Tobias walks with me. When we arrive at my corner, I stop, wondering if I should say something; offer to take Tobias out, maybe?

Yes, Arnie, that's kind of how this works.

"This is my turn here," I say instead.

Tobias sticks his hands into the pockets of his cargo shorts. "Well, hey, best of luck and all. Maybe we can get another drink before you disappear into the corporate world?"

Is Tobias asking me out? What is happening now? I panic,

because it's just not possible that Tobias Barrington is asking me, awkward Arnie Ferguson, out on a real date. This is some sort of pity drink, or like those times when someone says, "Let's get together soon," and they really mean "Not if I can help it."

"Uh, yeah, okay. Thanks again for the beer. That would be great. Having another drink together, I mean."

"Talk to you later."

"Bye," I say, mentally kicking myself but unable to force myself to ask for his phone number. Fear I'm misreading the situation is too strong to overcome.

Tobias sketches out a wave before jogging back across to the lake side of the street and taking the steps down toward the marina. When he reaches the bottom of the stairs, he glances back over his shoulder and catches me still watching him; my cheeks heat, but I manage to wave before turning away to begin walking up the hill, away from the glittering blue of Lake Washington toward my apartment. Away from the gorgeous and treacherous Tobias Barrington, whose cargo shorts must have been tailor-made, the way they hug his butt. And who is much nicer than I want him to be. Right?

He asked me out for a drink.

I don't intend on actually getting *involved* with Tobias Barrington, do I? I don't want to *date* Tobias.

No. No, I don't. I *don't*. No way. But, I think, chewing on the inside of my lip as I walk up the hill, this is absolutely a step in the right direction. Tobias is falling right in with my plan.

This is not the time to get sentimental.

But what if I want to?

This whole thing, it's supposed to be *boom*, revenge, and everything in my life will right itself, my course will become clear. But just like the night of that fateful party, the minute I'm around Tobias (with no sign of Charley) I'm fully focused on him. I want to get to know more about him—not just what I could possibly find on the internet. I want to know his secrets. I want to know if he likes pineapple on pizza, dogs or cats... top or bottom?

"Aargh," I groan.

I know I'm going to go out for another drink with him. I can't even stick to my own plan.

Crap.

EIGHT

Chapter Eight—Tobias

THE MINUTE ARNIE is up the hill and out of sight, I dig my phone out of my pocket and call Charley.

"Well?" Charley asks, instead of answering with a "Hello" like a civilized person. "How was it?"

I make my way to one of the benches overlooking Lake Washington and collapse onto it, my heart thumping against my chest as if I'd just finished running a marathon. "Fine?"

"Explain fine. Did you guys have drinks or not?"

"Yes. I took the day off—Dad was not happy—and I made sure I happened to be in the area when he got off work today."

"How'd you find that out?"

"I asked the owner, Gale."

"Isn't she someone's older sister? Eddie Harkness?" Charley asked.

"Yeah, but I think she's the black goat of the family."

"It's sheep, Tobias."

"Whatever."

"So, how'd it go?"

I hear soft noises across our connection, the clink of silverware and hushed conversation.

"Fine. I pretended to run into him, and we went to the Blue for a beer."

"And?"

"And what? We had a beer, talked for a little while, and then he had to go. I apologized for the coffee incident."

"Did you get his phone number?"

"No?"

"Tobias."

"I *know*" I half whine, "but I got nervous, and then I let the opportunity go by."

"What am I going to do with you?" I hear exasperation in his voice, but it's tempered with affection.

"I don't know. I guess we're going to be old bachelors together, and we'll sit at sidewalk cafes watching the rest of the world go by while we drink weak black coffee because we're lactose intolerant and talk about our farts."

"That was uncomfortably detailed."

"Am I wrong?"

"No," Charley grouses, "you probably aren't wrong. But I hope to god you are."

"What now?"

The line is silent for a moment. If it weren't for the hushed sounds on Charley's end, it would be easy to think we'd lost our signal.

"You need to get his damn phone number."

"Such a romantic," I tease.

"Ha, ha, ha. I've got to get back to being eye candy. You need a plan, my friend. And, I know I've been saying this for years, but maybe now you're finally listening: you need to cut your dad loose."

I sit on the bench for quite a while, the sun descending behind me and sending long shadows across the lake. On the other side of the water, the tall buildings of Bellevue glow with the attention until the sun's rays are too low to hit them any longer.

Tomorrow I'll come up with something to tell my father about why I took the day off, although something in my gut tells me I am finally ready for real change. Maybe I should go ahead and quit now. I could survive on my savings until April.

Tonight, though, I'm claiming victory. An unbidden smile stretches across my face; I may not have gotten Arnie's phone number, but I did get him to talk to me and go out for a drink. And it's not my imagination: there is a spark of *something* between us.

Charley is right. I need a plan—a life plan. One beginning with me making my own decisions about my life, like standing up to my dad. Maybe I haven't tried hard enough to get him to understand. I don't know; maybe he'll never listen to me— nothing in my past says he will. Andrew is an inherently selfish person. I'm okay with that, but I can't continue this path and blame him for my unhappiness.

I've never had any interest in property management, but the reality is, it's always been easier to go along with my father's wishes. There'd been a job for me when I graduated, not something all my friends had. But I'm starting to wonder if I didn't make things more difficult by delaying the inevitable.

Things might have been better if I'd stood up to my dad at the beginning instead of letting him have his way, letting him believe I was going to learn the business and take over Barrington Properties one day—when that's the last thing I want to do with my life.

Every day I spend there I hate it more. And with less than eight months until my birthday, I'm not sure if I'm going to last.

My thoughts swing back to Arnie Ferguson. Charley wanted to know what drew me to him, and all I can come up with is he's undefinable. It had been fun sitting on the patio with him and talking. I'd been nervous we wouldn't have anything to talk about, but Arnie is one of those guys who can talk about anything. It had been flattering he'd wanted to know about screenwriting, and now I feel bad I didn't ask what his dreams are, what job will take him away from the Buzz.

I'm not a risk taker—except maybe that time I invited Arnie to my room—and how am I supposed to bring that up? He's probably forgotten it ever happened. That had been a risk worth taking, and if I ever have another chance, I'll grab it.

I sigh.

I need to man up (a phrase I find distasteful but appropriate in this case). I need to do something about my life. If I want anything: a different career, Arnie Ferguson.

Charley is right, damn him.

NINE

Chapter Nine—Arnie

I SPEND the next day researching and occasionally cursing myself for not getting Tobias's phone number. When I'm not cursing, I'm reminding myself that my mission is *revenge*, not (boy)*friend*. I practice visualizing the words in neon on a big billboard in my head; maybe my mental self will walk by the sign and take note.

I pop open my laptop and search Barrington Properties to see if there's a job opening I'm remotely qualified for. After scrolling through the site, which has a magazine-like layout displaying a number of high-priced homes in Seattle and the suburbs, as well as commercial properties and land development opportunities, I find a link to employment at the very bottom. To my surprise, I find more than one job I'm qualified for (at least on my resume). There are more research-oriented jobs in real estate than I ever suspected. Of course, I've never looked before, but that's beside the point.

After a thirty-second wrestle with my conscience, I submit

my resume for an entry-level position at Barrington called "agent research assistant." Figuring I might be on to something, I search several other local companies and submit resumes to them as well. I hope Barrington Properties will call me back. It would be perfect: I'd get the job, get to know Tobias (in a revenge-y sort of way, of course), and then break his heart. Maybe not break; that sounds cruel. Maybe I'd just bend it a little.

I wonder suddenly—and why didn't this occur to me earlier —will Tobias think it strange if I land a job there? I'd never thought about that. It's becoming obvious there are more than a few tiny flaws in my plan. But, I reason, there's no law against applying for a job, even if a person is trying to right a cosmic wrong.

When I'm not obsessively refreshing my email to see if my job application has been reviewed, I'm storming the internet for more information about Tobias Barrington. There isn't much. A Facebook page is the only thing I find under Tobias's real name. He probably has a Grindr profile like sxyseattleboy, 2hot2tch96, or something equally obscure. This musing sends me down a rabbit hole of wondering what my Grindr name would be *if I had a profile on Grindr*... which I don't, so I really have no explanation for the wasted hours.

In the end, I settle on Ferg96_4U—if I were going to set up a profile, which I'm not. But does it sound too much like a presidential bumper sticker or the pop star? Probably.

No wonder I'm single.

A few hours later, I discover an ancient article from one of the local newspapers back when Tobias won the state championship in cross-country. God, I hate running. Although thinking about Tobias all hot and sweaty from a run gets me worked up, so maybe running isn't all that bad. But there's nothing else I can find.

The rest of the information I dig up is all about Tobias's father, Andrew Barrington. About his company and his philanthropic activity. There's even an article about what books the man reads, as if anyone cares. Although, judging by the number of comments at the end of the article, it seems people do care. Go figure.

I find several pictures of Andrew Barrington with a woman who is not Tobias's mother, but she's facing the other direction, and the way the pictures are shot it's hard to tell where they were taken. I peer at them, my nose nearly bonking against my screen: a hotel lobby, maybe, or a restaurant?

Is the elder Barrington's marriage on the rocks? He's been photographed with a much younger woman more than once. I doubt my mother knows about these pictures; she would have told me when we were shopping. I wonder if Tobias's father is having an affair and think it highly likely.

I've been sitting for hours now, cross-legged on the futon, and the heat from my laptop is making me sweaty. I adjust it on my lap, hoping to find a more comfortable position. The August heat wave Seattle is experiencing can go away anytime. And I wish, not for the first time, that we had air-conditioning in the studio. Something better than the plastic desk fan, anyway.

Forcing my attention back to my laptop, I manage to lose myself in "research" for another hour or so. I find, of course, a lot of information about Barrington Properties, most of which is financial statistics and growth things I'm not normally interested in, but I find myself reading it anyway.

My phone buzzes against my thigh, and I grab it. "Hi, Mom."

"Hey sweetie, how's it going? Anything on the job front?"

"Mom, it's been like two days since you saw me. No, I do not have a new job yet."

She laughs. "I know. I just like hearing the sound of your voice. I'm rooting for you!"

"As soon as I hear something, I'll let you know."

A blue jay flies up outside the window and lands on a branch of a cherry tree. It sees me watching it and caws chidingly at me before flying away in a huff. Just what I need, some jerk bird adding its opinion on my life.

"Do you want to come to dinner tonight?"

I grimace. I love my mother, but cooking is not her strong point. Neither is driving. We've come to an agreement about both.

"Do you mean meet somewhere?" I clarify.

"Yes, darling boy, I mean meet somewhere." She laughs again. "There's a new Peruvian place by my house. It's getting rave reviews."

"If we meet, can we not talk about my life?"

"I'm your mother; of course that's not possible."

Now I sigh. Peruvian sounds great. Maybe I need a dose of my mom's positivity. And maybe the restaurant will have air-conditioning. "Okay, dinner sounds great."

We agree to meet at seven thirty, which still gives me a few more hours to collect information about Tobias Barrington. Maybe I should've had another drink yesterday instead of running away; it would've been a lot easier to ask him questions outright. A lot easier to see if I could steer the conversation around to a party that happened years ago.

On a whim, I type in "screenwriting" and "screenwriters." The sheer amount of information is kind of overwhelming, and I lose myself in a Wikipedia post about the history of screenwriting.

One of my feet has fallen asleep. I stretch my leg out and curl my toes in anticipation of that horrible tingly feeling as the blood flow starts again.

I admit to myself that it isn't as if I don't want to have another drink with Tobias. I do; seeing him fits into my plan. But I'm not prepared. I need everything to be in place. That's why I refused his offer, I tell myself. Not because I'm a coward. And really, who am I kidding? I'm not heartbreak material—I'm more likely to trip and break my own dang heart. After all these years of thinking I hate Tobias Barrington, the truth is he makes my pulse race and my skin get all tingly.

No. I'm blaming the tingly on my foot being asleep. I absolutely am not having feelings. Any nascent feelings will be mentally stomped on.

Minutes after I click off the call from my mom, Duff's key rattles in the front door lock and my elusive roommate lets himself inside.

"Hey," I say.

"Hey," he says back.

Duff's wearing board shorts and a pair of flip-flops; a rucksack hangs over his bare shoulder. He seems leaner than normal and taut, probably from all the damn yoga and other exercise he loves. I'm lean from being naturally skinny, and any muscles I have come from making coffee and heaving bins of dishes back and forth.

"How was the lake?" I ask.

Tossing his backpack onto the floor, Duff pushes it under our futon chair and flops onto the cushions. Our studio is located in a 1920s-era building. Unlike modern studios, it isn't minuscule, but it is small for two people. We have room for a full-size futon couch and a chair that unfolds to become a twin-size sleeper, as well as a couple of bookshelves and a two-person table in one corner. I get the couch because I'm terminally single.

"It was great. Dude, it's hot out there, but I think it's hotter in here."

I have the fan pointing toward the futon. Reaching over, I move it slightly. Maybe it will bring the listless, slightly cooler, outside air inside. "I'm going to have dinner with Mom tonight, so I won't be home until nine or ten."

"Cool." Duff is resting his head against the back of the chair, and his eyes are half-shut. He looks tired.

"I talked to Gale. She's gonna introduce you to that Charley guy."

He opens his eyes to stare at me before letting his head flop backward again.

"Ugghh. You seriously still want to do this? I thought you'd give it up," Duff says to the ceiling.

A spark of irritation courses through my veins—regardless of my own feelings that it was a bad idea. Those I was keeping to myself. I *knew* Duff was going to keep trying to weasel out of our agreement. I'd brought him frozen peas when he needed them, and here he is reneging already.

Closing my laptop, I set it carefully on the floor, ignoring what he said. "Gale thinks you need to clean up a bit for Charley. Apparently, he likes 'preppy' guys. You need a haircut at least."

"Arnie," Duff whines.

"You promised," I retort, scowling.

"I was in pain, not in my right mind." He raises his head again. Seeing the look on my face, he grumbles, "Fine. What do you need me to do?"

"Your job is to distract Charley so I can swoop in and, uh, do my thing with Tobias. I saw him after work yesterday," I try to add in casually.

"Who?" Duff asks. "Charley or Tobias?"

"Tobias. I kind of ran into him after I got off work. He actually asked me for a drink. The whole thing was very weird."

Mostly because the list of people who've asked me for a drink is still something I can count on only two hands.

Very slowly, Duff turns his head so he is full-on staring at me now instead of the ceiling. He has a look in his eyes that I identify as extreme disbelief.

"He what?" Duff asks.

"He asked me if I wanted... no, he asked if he could buy me a drink." I can't remember Tobias's exact words; the heat must be affecting my brain. Or something.

Duff snorts, or maybe it's a gasp of exasperation. "Why are we going through these shenanigans if the guy has already asked you out? Isn't that exactly what you want?"

I glare fiercely across the room. Duff stares back with equal fervor, eyes narrow and eyebrows near his hairline.

"He didn't ask me out. He asked if I wanted a drink. I was hot and sweaty from working in the dish pit and probably looked like I was going to pass out. And I did want a drink, so we went and had one, but it isn't the same thing."

"Your logic isn't even circular—it's a wavy line."

It doesn't help my mood to have Duff echoing my own thoughts. I *am* a loser. I know I've gotten myself all twisted up with this idea of revenge, but I'm going through with it. So there.

"People don't just randomly offer to buy other people drinks, Arnie."

Duff is back to staring at the ceiling again, so he doesn't see my blush, thank goodness.

"Maybe Tobias Barrington does! Maybe he goes around town offering everyone he sees a drink. Especially if it's really hot and they look thirsty." I throw up my hands. "I don't want to talk about it anymore. Just promise me you'll get yourself a haircut before the block party next week. I guess that's when Gale's going to introduce you to Charley Hunter."

The block party is a huge event held every August on Capitol Hill. Live bands, food stalls, contortionists, clowns, a parade—not an official Pride parade, but one that makes up for the fact the official one moved to downtown, making it no fun anymore—it's a blast. As much of an introvert as I am, the block party is something I try not to miss.

"What do Charley Hunter and the block party have to do with each other?"

"You and Charley are going to get together there, I think."

"This is ridiculous."

"It's not," I insist. Deep down, I know full well my plan is ludicrous, but... I've set everything in motion, and I feel for the first time in years as if I'm actually taking action—making a plan and following through. So what if it's a ridiculous plan?

"It *is*. But whatever."

AFTER MULLING over my life for the rest of the afternoon, I almost miss the bus that will drop me close to the restaurant where I'm meeting my mom. I can't miss the bus; the prospect of her coming to pick me up is more frightening than almost anything.

I shiver at the thought of riding with her, even though the apartment is warm and humid, while I quickly change clothes. Duff is asleep, and I spare a moment to worry about him. It looks to me like he's lost weight—and he's already too thin; I don't care if photographers like his looks. I feel very protective of my best friend.

As I stuff my wallet into the back pocket of my jeans, Duff partially opens his eyes. He has pretty eyes, a kind of chocolaty-caramely color. Not for the first time, I wish we were attracted to each other; it would make things much simpler.

I open my mouth to say something, to maybe ask if he's

doing okay, but he shuts his eyes again, pretending he's asleep. Fine, we'll talk later then.

Over the years, I've definitely been the one who relied on him rather than the other way around. We've been friends a long time, through thick and thin, and I've never once worried if I could ask him for help or advice. He's always been solid.

I'm a little worried about him now, but I'm not sure what to do about it. Once I get this whole Tobias Barrington thing out of the way, I'll shift my attention to Duff.

TEN

Chapter Ten—Tobias

"I'VE HAD one of the staff post the job description already."

I look up at the ceiling, then over my dad's shoulder out the window to the magnificent view behind him, and then I count backward from twenty before I reply, hoping to calm myself down.

"Dad—" I begin.

"How many times do I have to remind you to either call me Andrew or Mr. Barrington when we're at the office?"

I breathe in a gallon of air through my nose and blow it out through my mouth. Less than eight months until my birthday. I can do this. However, the tiny stream of calm I gain by counting backward and deep breathing isn't nearly deep enough.

"Andrew, I don't want an assistant. Especially if that person is basically hired to do my job because I'm bad at it."

"Tobias, don't be dramatic. The new hire will help everyone in the office, not just you."

As far as I can tell, it's my father who is making things difficult, but pointing that out would just lead to another lecture.

"I've decided to expand your role." Andrew leans back in his desk chair, his expression close to avid. "You represent a demographic Barrington would like to garner more of. In the next months, as we get closer to the end of the year, you will be representing the company at meetings and networking events where there are others like you. With your involvement, they're more likely to list their houses and properties with us. It's a win-win situation."

"They?"

I'm going to make him say it. If Andrew Barrington plans to pimp me out to groups like the Gay Business Association, I'm forcing him to say the words. *Word.* I'd come out to my parents when I was eighteen—a few days after the infamous party, actually—and my announcement had been met with complete silence. My mom patted me on the shoulder and said something about shopping, and my dad hadn't said anything at all. It was as if my words had disappeared between my lips and their ears. They didn't want to hear them; therefore I hadn't said them.

I'd bet my inheritance Andrew read something recently about gay people having disposable income. If "the gays" can make him money, Andrew can bring himself to acknowledge my sexuality.

Just another reason to quit working for Barrington Properties and get on with my own life.

"People like you."

My dad shifts, not meeting my angry stare, his desk chair squeaking under his weight.

"Like me, Dad—I mean, Andrew? I think you need to clarify. White? Male? Mid-twenties? I don't understand."

Andrew's lips twist, and disdain drips from his words. "Homosexuals, Tobias."

How hard was that? "You know what? I don't want to be the token gay representing Barrington. And, for your information, there is no way I am your only gay employee."

"Get over yourself. This is about money. That's what's important here."

I'm trapped. I have access to more money than most people in the world, and it traps me in a life I hate. They aren't golden handcuffs—they're platinum, and I can't rip them off just yet. As long as Sarah-Michelle is at home, I will stay there. Our parents' toxicity is just too much to deal with alone. All our lives, they've used us as foils in their little games. I am so sick of it.

"Carly has a list of events you'll be attending over the next few weeks. Stop by her desk on the way out."

And now I've been dismissed. Wonderful. But there's nothing to say, no protest I can make that would make my dad suddenly understand me or see me for the person I really am. I'm not ready to make my move. I'm not ready to tell him to fuck off. And a small part of me wants him to be proud of me, to support my dreams.

I do have a plan: I'm going to write an incredible screenplay and sell it to Hollywood. I want to shove my success in my dad's face—prove to him I have my own value.

The screenplay thing is probably a pipe dream, I know. Screenwriting is an intensely competitive field. But I want to try, and if I fail, it's my failure to own, nothing to do with Andrew Barrington.

"THANKS, CARLY," I say when she hands me the appointment sheet.

"Of course, Tobias. I'll send it to your email too."

Back in my own office, I shut the door behind myself and slump in my desk chair.

Eight months. I can do it.

Once a month or so, I make my way to the U District and walk south down the Ave. The street is actually University Way, but it was nicknamed "the Ave" back in 1919, and the name stuck. The Ave is one street off the university campus and is home to a multitude of student-oriented businesses, restaurants, and other services.

About halfway between 45th and Pacific is the Selznick Building, my freedom. The building was left to me in a trust from my maternal grandmother, and when I turn twenty-five it will become mine. I don't plan on selling; I want to use the income the building generates to fund the next step in my dream of screenwriting and maybe making movies of my own someday. Who says a boy can't dream big?

Freedom is so close I can almost taste it.

The Selznick houses a coffee shop, a brewery, and a flower shop at street level. Above are two floors of apartments, six on each floor. They're always rented out, with a waiting list of students who want to live close to, but not on, campus. It feels a bit weird knowing I'm close to becoming a landlord, but if it means I'll be free to live the life I want, I want to take on the responsibility.

Eight months. I can do that. Eight months and I'll have the freedom to take screenwriting classes in person and see if I really have what it takes to write movies—and maybe produce them too. I want to write off-the-wall stuff featuring LGBTQIA people—and other marginalized people—living their lives.

Time will seem to pass faster if the next eight months include Arnie Ferguson. I spin around in my chair so I can look out the window. We've had one drink together, and I'm hopeful there will be more.

Charley is right, Arnie is a little different, but his different meshes with my awkward. At least I think so. Arnie makes me laugh, and our short date was fun—even better at the end when Arnie glanced back over his shoulder at me. I hadn't imagined the pink tinge to his cheeks.

Chapter Eleven—Arnie

THE BUS LETS me off right across the street from the restaurant Mom picked out. The Taste of the Andes is located in an old house on a busy corner in north Seattle. The building is cute, two stories tall and painted a garish orange I immediately like. Unfortunately, my hopes for air-conditioning are rapidly diminishing, as the screened windows are wide open. As I push through the entrance, a waft of spicy yumminess greets me, and my mouth starts to water. My mom made a good choice.

About half the tables are full this evening, but my mom hasn't arrived yet. The waitperson seats me at an open table near one of the windows before quickly returning with two glasses of ice water.

I make myself comfortable and gaze around at my fellow patrons. People watching is a hobby of mine. I like to observe other people and make up stories in my head about their lives. For instance, the couple in the far corner from me seem like they are on a first date. Their outfits don't match: the guy is wearing jeans and a T-shirt, whereas the young woman, in her dress and heels, seems to have expected something more than a casual outing.

Oftentimes when I'm watching people, it's to sort out where I've gone wrong—if that's even possible. Is there a life-instruction manual I've never been privy to? It sure feels like it. Why can't you answer "Shitty" when someone asks, "How's your day going"? Why are you expected to say "Great"? What's the point of asking the question if it isn't going to be answered honestly? I have questions.

Too many times to count, my parents were called by my teachers with complaints about my behavior. Before the divorce, there'd been a big family argument when my mom wanted to take me to counseling and "the asshole," as Mom now refers to my father, refused, saying whatever was wrong with me, it was too late to fix and she needed to stop coddling me.

Before my father uttered those words, I'd never considered something might be wrong with me, but even now, ten years or so later, they still rattle around in my brain, making me anxious and self-conscious. Maybe there is something wrong with me, something that makes it hard for me to read social cues—like is it my imagination, or is Tobias truly interested in me? Oh, and isn't that sweet. I watch as jeans guy reaches across the table to hold the woman's hand, and she looks happy about it. I release a little sigh, quickly imagining a beautiful wedding for them, followed by bliss and all that.

"Heya, sweetie."

I've been so caught up envisioning the couple's wedding, I didn't notice my mother's arrival. I stand, ready to pull out her chair, but she's too fast for me, dragging it out and sitting down before I can react.

"Hey, Mom."

"Sorry I'm late. I got stuck in the worst traffic. If the city changes one more street to one way or adds one more damn bike lane, I'm going to stage a protest."

I nod. It's true, Seattle is more difficult to navigate these days.

"But whatever, I'm here now. Let's order."

While our dinner is being prepared, I wonder how long it will take Mom to bring up my future (as yet nonexistent) job plans. I set a mental timer, but it hasn't even begun ticking when she says, "So, I want to hear more about your plans. I'm so proud of you, Arnie, for stepping out of your comfort zone and trying something new. It's hard to do, and I know you like Gale and most of the other people at the coffee shop." She qualifies her comment with a smile.

I shift in my seat, the praise making me uncomfortable. "Mom, don't get all excited. Even with the new clothes—and thank you again—I probably won't land a new job. I suck at interviews."

She leans forward, eyes sparkling with excitement. "I can help you. We can role play."

"What?"

My mother has not just suggested role play. I cannot handle that idea. Most especially because role play is something I read about in romance novels. Role play is not something you do with your mother. Wait. Is there... mommy kink? I grab my ice water and chug it down, suddenly thirsty like the dude who'd ridden through the desert on an incognito equine. Yes, I was born to a woman who had '70s music on replay throughout my childhood —and still does. Along with many others, I can recite all the words to "A Horse with No Name" by America, as well as all the songs by Yusuf Islam. It's a gift, one that keeps giving and giving.

"Are you okay?" Mom asks. "I would be totally willing to help you role play. I could play the strict interviewer."

I cough as my water goes down the wrong pipe, and the waiter hurries over. In fact, now all eyes in the restaurant are on me as I cough and choke until the ice cube dislodges itself.

"Fine," I rasp out, "just fine."

"Well, what do you think about role play?"

The waiter hasn't left our table yet and, unfortunately, I witness his expression at my mother's words and accidentally catch his eye. I'm never going to be able to come back to this place, no matter how good the food is.

"I'll bring more water," Stephan the waitperson says quickly and walks away, his shoulders shaking.

I look up at the ceiling, then back at my mother, who is patiently waiting for my answer.

"No, Mom, thank you for the offer. If I get an interview, I think I'll practice in front of the mirror. And can you please not use the phrase 'role play'?"

"I can play a really stern boss."

"Mom!"

Now she laughs. I narrow my eyes at her.

"Just kidding, Arnie."

The rest of our meal goes much more smoothly, although I still can't look Stephan in the eye. We share a plate of papas rellenas and arroz con pollo, followed by arroz con leche for dessert. We don't talk much while we eat, our only sounds little gasps of delight as we taste everything.

Sitting back in my chair, I groan and rub my stomach. "I'm sooo full. I'm on a food high; nothing can bring me down."

My mom smiles, and it's a different kind of smile. It's slightly unsure, not an expression I'm used to seeing from her. I have a premonition—or, at least, I'm abruptly wary. The thought occurs to me that maybe she didn't invite me to dinner merely to grill me about job opportunities.

I narrow my eyes at her, trying to figure out what's going on inside her head. It's never worked. As much as I believe life would be a lot easier if I could read minds, I've never made it happen. People mostly just think I have something in my eye.

I open my mouth to ask what is going on, but before I can say anything, Mom blurts out, "I'm seeing someone. His name is Will, he's a dentist, divorced, and has two daughters around your age." She rattles off the list as if she's trying to sell him to me. Career: check. Kids: check. Divorced: check. The divorced part is good, because I don't want Mom having an affair. I don't want her seeing anyone, do I?

The delicious food sits heavy in my stomach now. Who is this Will-the-dentist? He's probably some serial killer. How does she know the guy is for real? How did they meet? What if he's a scammer trying to take advantage of her, lying in wait to steal all her savings and leave her brokenhearted? I briefly imagine my mother on OkCupid or Tinder, but luckily my brain won't let me go any further than the front page of the website.

"Why didn't you tell me about him before? How long have you been seeing him? Why are you telling me about him now?" I ask.

I try not to sound upset, but I am. I am *really* upset, and the thing is, I know my mom isn't fooled and my reaction is exactly why she hasn't told me until now.

I hate being this predictable. The part of me that has been busy applying for jobs, getting a new wardrobe, and thinking about Tobias as more than a revenge plot points out that my mom deserves happiness. When I think this, I almost feel a puzzle piece fall into place inside me. Both of us deserve happiness.

Mom leans across the table, holding my gaze. "I want to introduce you. I'm hoping we can meet for dinner, maybe this coming weekend or the next?"

"Dinner?"

"Yes, dinner, Arnie. Will and I would like to introduce—we want our kids to meet. But first I want you to meet him."

"Mom." I want her to know I'm happy for her—but we've been a team for so long. Rita and Arnie against the world.

"Arnie, think about it, please? For me? I know it's a lot to take in, and change is difficult, but I think you'll like him. I like him. A lot."

My mom's hazel eyes, almost the same shade as mine, are wide and pleading. I want to say no. I want to allow myself to be angry. But I can't, so I don't.

I'm twenty-four and don't want to share my mother. Way to be a grown-up.

Silence stretches between us. It's intruded on only by the clatter of silverware against dinner plates and hum of conversation from the diners around us.

"Okay," I agree.

She blinks at me. "Okay?"

"Okay, I will meet this guy."

I know I'll hate Will, but I'm going to try to be polite. And then I'm going to research the shit out of him. If he has even a hair out of place, I'm going to make sure Mom knows about it.

But first I'm going to attempt to like this skanky Will guy for her, because she deserves to meet someone new, someone who will treat her right.

I LET Mom drive me home, clearly too stunned by her little news bomb to think straight. The streets of Seattle are still crowded, but at least they're navigable. Mom only swears and shakes her fist at another driver once. At my place she pulls into the drop-off zone in front. The drive had been quiet, both of us thinking about life changes, I guess.

"I love you, Arnie." Her soft lips brush against my cheek, Mom's standard peck goodbye.

"I love you too, Mom."

"I'll call, or text you, about dinner."

"Great," I manage, with a barely suppressed sense of doom looming over me as I climb out of the car.

I stand on the sidewalk for a minute, watching until her brake lights disappear from sight. The sun is just beginning to set, and somehow that seems appropriate. Instead of climbing the stairs to my apartment, I turn and follow the sidewalk down the hill to the lake.

The shiny office buildings on the far side of Lake Washington glitter back at me, reflecting the pink, purple, and orange glow of the sunset. The empty bench by the marina beckons. I cross the street and claim it, then watch as the sky puts on a magnificent display before fading to a dark blue and black canvas of stars. The sailboats moored in their slips clank and shuffle against each other, darker silhouettes against the evening sky. Beginning or end, it's hard for me to tell.

TWELVE

Chapter Twelve—Arnie

OVER THE NEXT FEW DAYS, I check my email obsessively. I can't stop myself. Finally, lurking among newsletters, special offers, and amazing offers from Nigerian princes with no heirs if only I will cough up all of my financial information, is an email with the subject line, "Thank you for your application." My heart starts to race, and my hand actually shakes as I drag my mouse down and click on the email.

I have the studio to myself; Duff left early for his morning yoga. Or maybe it's some other class by now. I have a hard time keeping track of his whereabouts. Still, I make a note to myself to corner him the next time I see him.

But what Duff is doing, or, rather, who he is with, doesn't matter as long as he sticks to our agreement. He's agreed to distract Charley Hunter—although I'm 99 percent sure that Charley and Tobias aren't a "thing" at all, only friends. I mentally kick myself for not asking Tobias about Charley the other day, although I'm a little unclear on how I'd actually go about doing that.

"So, Tobias, are Charley's intentions honorable?" No.

"Tobias, are you really dating Charley Hunter?" Definitely not; that makes it seem like I don't like Charley. I remind myself that I don't.

I return to reading my emails.

"Mr. Arnold Ferguson, we are pleased to have received your application for research assistant at Barrington Properties. We'd like to set up a phone interview to discuss your qualifications. A list of available days and times is provided below. Please respond with your first and second choice, and we will confirm..."

I shriek into my pillow so I won't scare the neighbors. Then I shriek again for good measure. My heart is pounding now, with a mix of fear and excitement. I actually have an interview—a phone interview, but an interview nonetheless.

With trembling fingers, I scroll through the message twice more, making sure I don't miss any important information, then I read it thoroughly a fourth time before clicking Reply. I select the first day possible for the phone call.

I'm sure they've made some mistake, gotten my resume mixed up with another's, but if Barrington Properties is going to let me get a toe in the door, I'm going to take it. It's exactly what I want, right?

MY LUNCHTIME SHIFT at the Buzz is a blur due to my excitement over my upcoming interview. Even if it's only a phone call, it's *something*. Sweat drips down the back of my neck, and my T-shirt is sticking to my back and chest as I plow through the pile of lunch dishes and ceramic coffee mugs as quickly as I can. The entire city of Seattle decided today was the day to have lunch out, and I've been relegated to the dish pit for what feels like hours—but finally the stack of dishes has shrunk to the point where I can head back out into the dining area for one last check before I leave.

A familiar silhouette catches my attention. Tobias is sitting alone at a table near the door. He's sipping some sort of iced drink and looking at his phone. Just as I'm deciding if I should flee back to the dish pit or sneak out the front door, he looks up and smiles at me. I can't blame the temperature for the flush that heats my cheeks, or for the tingly feeling in my stomach.

"Hi, Arnie," Tobias calls out.

When Tobias says my name, it doesn't sound like a goofy name, it sounds like my favorite dark chocolate. Tobias's voice latches on to something unnameable in my stomach and pulls me, damp T-shirt and all, across the room to where he's sitting. I think about what Duff said the other night, that people don't randomly ask people if they want to get a drink. I think about the fact that I haven't seen Tobias since then, and that it's nice to see him this afternoon. More than nice. Like, really nice.

Tobias smiles up at me, rendering me speechless for a second. I'm really not very good at this whole luring-in-for-revenge thing. Maybe I wasn't cut out for a life of crime.

"Hi, Tobias. Um, how's it going?"

Tobias's smile broadens, and his eyes crinkle at the corners. Dang, he's going to have sexy-assed smile lines when he's older.

Someone behind me clears their throat, but I ignore them.

"Good. Even better now," Tobias replies.

"Oh yeah? Why? Did you win the lottery?"

Ugh. Tobias is already rich; he doesn't need the lottery.

Tobias's gaze flickers past me. I glance over my shoulder and see my nemesis, Charley Hunter, standing behind me, clearing his throat again.

"Oh, sorry," I say, automatically moving aside so Charley

can sit down. I wonder if Gale would fire me if I accidentally poured hot coffee in his lap.

Tobias's dark brows draw together.

"Sorry," I say again, "I didn't mean to get in your way."

Charley looks me up and down in a very appraising manner and says, "No worries."

Ugh. I scowl at him and slip back behind the counter. They aren't dating. Charley is too much of a dick for someone as nice as Tobias. Eli glances over at me from where he's standing over by the brew station, his eyes full of questions I won't answer at the moment. I shake my head, clock out, and head into the back to drop off my dirty apron before leaving.

I'm not supposed to like Tobias. For years I haven't liked him. I hate him for treating me like so much garbage after the party, right? But I do like him.

One minute we'd been naked and bumping private bits together, and the next I was in the front yard. A painful memory on many levels, but the worst was the lingering feeling that I'd made a fool of myself.

Up until my impromptu coffee shower a few weeks ago, Tobias hadn't acknowledged my existence. We don't run in the same social circles, and if I did happen to see him around town, he made no indication that he remembered our night of passion —or me. I'm starting to think I may have been wrong about that. Tobias is shy. Maybe he didn't know how to say hi to *me*. Huh, way to figure something out, Arnie.

Remarkably, I've never been electrocuted (really, with my history it's a surprise), but after that night with Tobias, I think I know what the shock might feel like. Sure, there'd been fumbling—I'd never "gone all the way" before that night, and I'd been a little drunk—but I've never forgotten the slide of our skin, his smooth chest against mine, the kissing. It had been magical.

Pointedly looking the opposite direction from where Tobias and Charley are sitting, I push out through the front door to head home. I'm angry and feel out of my depth. Charley managed to muddy the good feelings I had from the other day with Tobias. Which is fine. I don't want good feelings.

THIRTEEN

Chapter Thirteen—Tobias

GLARING AT MY BEST FRIEND, I demand, "What'd you do that for?"

Charley smirks. "What?" For once, I'm actually mad at him. "Scare him away."

"If he scares away that easily, he's not worth your time. You need a guy who'll stay and fight for you."

I eye him, wondering if he's talking about Arnie or if he's thinking about his ex. Charley hides behind a wall of snark and sarcasm. It can be difficult to know what's really going on in his head.

"Knock it off. You're supposed to be helping, not chasing him away."

Movement catches my attention. Arnie is pushing his way out the door, very purposefully not looking in our direction. Charley follows my gaze.

"Go after him." Charley nods his head toward the swiftly departing figure. "Catch up with him and tell him I'm a jerk or something, then ask him out. See, I helped." He waves for me to run after Arnie.

I don't think twice about it. I jump up from my chair and dash out of the café.

"Arnie!" I call out.

His shoulders stiffen. I know he's heard me, but he doesn't turn around or stop walking—although he may have slowed infinitesimally.

I break into a jog in order to catch up with him.

"Stop for a sec," I beg.

Arnie stops, slowly turning to face me.

"I'm sorry Charley was a jerk," I blurt out.

Arnie shrugs. "He's your friend, not mine."

He's right, but I'm still sorry Charley upset him. "Are you going to the block party next week?"

A wary expression flits across his handsome face. I shouldn't have asked Charley to meet me at the Buzz for coffee. He's becoming a liability. He's going to hear it from me if he's ruined all my work from last week.

"Maybe," he allows. "Probably. Why?"

"We could meet up? I've heard the lineup is great this year. And there's going to be a beer garden."

Arnie glances at me, then looks out toward the lake, sunshine glints against the lenses of his glasses. He seems to be having an internal debate with himself. I want to push, but I stay silent. Please, please, please.

"Okay. I'll meet up with you," he agrees, finally.

Internally I'm jumping up and down, but all I say is, "Great." And then, "How about we exchange phone numbers, just in case?"

"Yeah." He nods. "Good idea."

. . .

BACK AT THE COFFEE SHOP, Charley is waiting at the table for me. I slide into my seat, a big, goofy grin on my face.

"Success?"

"We're meeting at the block party, and I got his phone number."

"Nicely done."

"Now what do I do?"

Charley's bright blue eyes light up with amusement. "Now comes the hard part: you get to know him."

"I have to say, it seems kind of weird to try and get to know a guy when we already, um, slept together."

"I'm pretty sure there was no sleeping. And... it happened years ago. You're different people now."

Gale, the owner of the Buzz, emerges from a short hallway that likely leads to restrooms and an office or break room. I see when she spots us sitting here. She immediately changes direction, heading our way. We both know Gale from the neighborhood. She's a bit older than us, maybe four or five years, but the Madison/Capitol Hill neighborhood is a tight community. All the kids grow up playing on the same soccer teams, and many go to the same few private schools.

"I'm calling in that favor," Gale says when she reaches us.

"What favor? I don't owe you a favor," I squeak. Gale is more than a little intimidating.

"I'm talking to Danny Ocean here." Gale pats Charley's shoulder. I don't know why she calls Charley that. He looks nothing like George Clooney.

Charley sighs and rolls his eyes. "What?"

"I'm setting you up with Duff Cleveland. He's going to ask you out, and you're going to say yes."

"Duff? Gale, Duff is... he's hot enough, but..."

"Thanks." Gale starts back toward the counter. "Stop in tomorrow when he's working."

Charley slumps in his seat, glaring after her.

"What was that about?"

"I owe Gale a favor."

"I gathered that much. Duff Cleveland, though? Do you even know him?" I'm dying to ask what favor he owes Gale, but I don't. I can hazard a guess, though; it has something to do with Charley's ex.

Charley stalls by taking a sip of his not-so-iced-anymore coffee. "I've run into him few times. He's a model. And here, of course."

I cave and ask, "Are you going to tell me why you owe her a favor?"

Charley aggressively sips his coffee. "Nope."

FOURTEEN

Chapter Fourteen—Tobias

ANOTHER DAY AT BARRINGTON PROPERTIES, another brain cell lost—or, at least, I feel that much closer to turning into an actual zombie. I'm not sure what I dislike more, the condescending way my father speaks to me or the secret glances other staffers and agents in the office share between each other but think I don't notice. Because yeah, I really need that on top of everything else.

I need to just take the fallout and move on with my life. Sarah-Michelle is graduating high school next spring and, unlike my choices at eighteen, she has the world at her feet. Dad largely ignores her as long as her grades are good. Sarah-Michelle and our mother have spent a lot of the past spring and early summer traveling to campuses across the US, with the trip to LA coming up in a couple weeks. I hope she picks a college as far away as possible. I also suspect the trips are an excuse for Olivia to go on shopping sprees of epic proportions. She doesn't care where Sarah-Michelle goes to college, as long as there is boutique shopping.

Charley is right to berate me for continuing to put up with my family: still living in the big house on the hill, letting my father dictate everything from the clothes I wear (suit required) to the food on my plate in the evening. I know this... but, I remind myself, I promised myself I wouldn't abandon my sister. I have a calendar set in my smartphone with a countdown to my birthday. All I know is, it's not soon enough.

After April, if Sarah-Michelle chooses to go to the Savannah College of Art and Design or MIT—Savannah is too arty for Andrew, he has some long-standing grudge against MIT, and neither school has the kind of shopping Olivia wants—I'll be able to help her out financially if she needs it. What isn't covered by scholarships, anyway. Sarah-Michelle is the brains between us.

Instead of getting anything productive done, I spend the afternoon wondering about the different facets of Arnie. I don't know him well yet, but he makes me laugh, and I know he's fierce. Other than Charley and Sarah-Michelle, he's the only person I've ever told about wanting to learn screenwriting, and he seemed genuinely interested.

I want to know more about him. I want to find out what his dreams are. I want to know if the connection I feel goes both ways. I'm guessing it does. But I'm not sure. I thought he hated me... but now, like yesterday, I'm pretty sure he's thinking about me the same way I do about him.

When the clock on my computer finally turns over to five o'clock, I shut down the open programs and power it off. My phone rings just as I'm deciding whether or not to wear my suit jacket home. Not my desk phone; the last time that rang was when dinosaurs roamed the earth. Reaching into my pocket, I pull out my phone and glance at the screen. It's Arnie. My heart rate picks up.

"Hello."

"Oh, uh, hi, Tobias?" He sounds a little breathless.

"Yes, this is Tobias." I chuckle, because we only just exchanged numbers. Did he think I would give him the wrong one?

"Okay, uh, good. This is Arnie, Arnie Ferguson."

I want to laugh, but I don't. I can totally relate to Arnie's nerves. "Hey, Arnie, how's it going?"

"Yeah, good, thanks, so youknowthatblockpartythingthisweekend?"

I have no idea what he's just said, but I'm pretty sure he's about to hyperventilate.

"Slow down. You're talking too fast. I'm having a hard time understanding you."

"I know. I'm sorry. I hate talking on the phone. Deep breath, okay. Um..." While Arnie tries to pull himself together, I wander over to look out my office window. Barrington Properties occupies its own building on Eastlake, and I have a view of Lake Union looking out toward Puget Sound. It's one of the only things I like about this job. Maybe the only thing I like.

"Anyway, about the block party. It turns out"—Arnie sucks in a breath before releasing a gusty sigh and continuing—"my mother wants to have dinner with me that night; I get to meet the new boyfriend. I'd tell her I was busy, but then I'd get like the thousand-question interrogation about what I was doing that was more important, 'especially since we already talked about it.'" He ends the sentence in a falsetto voice, making me grin.

From Arnie's tone, I figure he's just learned about his mom's new boyfriend. He also sounds bummed out about missing the block party. I'm disappointed too; I was looking forward to spending the evening with him. I do my best to shove that aside and not be whiny.

"It's fine. We can reschedule," I say with some difficulty. Looking forward to going to the block party with Arnie has been the only thing that's kept me dragging myself out of bed the past couple of days. Or... "Or, if you wanted to, we could meet earlier and check out the first bands." That would be something to redeem the day.

"We both know the good stuff happens later."

This is true. All the funky things that make the block party what it is happen in the evening. "I could tag along for dinner," I find myself blurting. "I'm usually pretty good at impressing the parents."

Silence.

"Or not. It was a silly thought." Hoo boy, I'm the one taking deep breaths now. Outside, over the glittering water, a float-plane soars upward, then dips down before regaining altitude and disappearing in the distance, taking my two-second good mood with it.

"You'd be willing to go on a... meet my mother on... I can't even say it!" Arnie's voice is breathless and squeaky.

A chuckle escapes me, because it is a bit weird to offer to meet someone's parent out of the blue. Like I'm throwing myself at him. But Arnie's sputtering is sweet, not malicious, and there are other days we could meet. It doesn't have to be Saturday.

Before I can figure out how to take back my words, though, Arnie says, "It could work... but I'm warning you ahead of time, my mom is... a force of nature. And she—well, never mind about that. If you're sure. Are you sure? Because you're going to get the ninth degree if I bring you along—or maybe, because of the dentist, you won't? This is an angle I hadn't considered before. It could work. Maybe this is a good way for you to meet my mom; she'll be so distracted by the dentist you can just kind of slip in, and maybe we'll manage to have a normal dinner. I haven't exactly said anything about you to her—I mean, since we aren't really anything. Oh my god—" His voice rises as a higher level of panic sets in.

"Arnie," I interrupt, "I'm sure about joining you, or I wouldn't have offered. We can just be casual."

"We'll have to take the bus," he continues without responding to me. "I don't have a car. Great, taking you to meet my mom and the skank dentist, and we have to ride the bus." He sounds so glum I can't help but laugh.

"Arnie," I break in, "I have a car. Did you say 'skank dentist'?"

"Ohhh, this gets even better. I invite you to meet my mother and her new-to-me boyfriend, and you have to drive? This, *this* is why I need to get my life together. Did you hear me say the ninth degree? It's worse than the third degree by a factor of three. She will leave no stone unturned. Yes, I said skank dentist." Another gusty sigh floats across our connection. "I really need to stop thinking of him that way, or I'll accidentally say it when I meet him."

"I don't mind driving. What time do we need to be there?"

"Reservations are for seven, at a place in Lynnwood. Um, we could meet a little earlier, and I can take you out for a drink as a bribe?"

I smile. My reflection in the window smiles back at me. "How about I pick you up at five?"

"That sounds great. I gotta go, so, uh, see you on Saturday. Wait, on second thought, let's plan for a drink *after* dinner. I'm sure we'll both need one."

"Okay. So six thirty, then? And Arnie..."

"Yeah?"

"I need your address."

He rattles off his address, then says, "Tobias?"

"Yeah?"

"I can't believe you're agreeing to meet my mother. You don't have to. We can reschedule. Have I mentioned my mom knew your dad in college?"

I don't want to reschedule; I've committed to it.

"I'll see you Saturday," I say, wondering how Arnie's mom knew Andrew but figuring I'll learn soon enough.

FIFTEEN

Chapter Fifteen—Arnie

IT'S Saturday before I know it. I've tried not to obsess (too much) about the dinner, and until yesterday I had a distraction: nailing my interview with Barrington. I was surprised—okay, stunned—when they called back the day after the phone screen and said they wanted me to come in for a follow-up. I spent every free minute scanning a ton of online articles about how to prepare for an interview, and I even sort of practiced in front of the bathroom mirror—not once thinking about the idea of role play with *my mother*.

I think the interview went well. I even texted my mom and told her about it, with the caveat I'm not talking about it at dinner: not a word is to be mentioned. I'm not superstitious (although Duff might argue that point), but I don't want my mom getting excited about a new job when all I've done so far is talk to a woman about research techniques, my knowledge (or lack thereof) of the real estate business, and the question I hate the most, "Where do you see yourself in five years."

That question bothers me. Did the interviewer expect me to say I long to work in an office environment for the rest of my life—that I dream of nothing but mindless meetings and copy machines? I think they still have those things. Gah.

It's a good thing Duff was out doing his Duff thing for most of the week. I don't need him giving me advice. Especially since he already thinks my plan is ridiculous. When he did come home Friday night, I pretended to be asleep. I don't think he was fooled, but I don't want to talk about it.

I'm really not superstitious. Maybe I make the effort to not step on cracks and not break mirrors, but I've only tossed salt over my shoulder once (and I'm pretty sure it was the wrong shoulder). I guess I just like to think that if there is such a thing as luck, I want the good stuff. I think I need it.

Saturday morning, I end up spilling to Duff about Tobias and me meeting Mom and her new-to-me skank boyfriend (cannot actually call him that, I remind myself) for dinner.

"So," I begin, "I guess I don't need you to hang out with Charley tonight. You're off the hook."

"That's a relief." His shoulders actually sag.

"Sorry. I shouldn't have asked you to do that."

"Nah, it's fine. I just have other plans, and Charley Hunter is not a part of them."

"You've been out a lot this week. Is there something I should know about? Or someone?" I'm dying of curiosity, but Duff plays his love life close to his chest. I hardly ever meet his dates. They get clingy, and Duff shows them the door, so to speak.

He's in the kitchenette with his back to me, making one of his revolting healthy shakes. His shoulders stiffen, and I know I've strayed too close to the truth. There might actually be someone he is serious about.

"Nope," he says.

Okay, subject closed.

. . .

IT'S EARLY SATURDAY EVENING. Duff left for parts unknown a few hours ago, and I'm on my own trying to decide what to wear to dinner. After changing my mind six or ten times, I decide on a pair of slacks and one of the new shirts my mom bought for me. I check myself out in the mirror. Do I look good enough to hang out with Tobias Barrington of the Seattle Barringtons? Turning a bit, I check my backside; the answer is yes. The slacks definitely make my butt look good, and I mentally thank Brad, the helpful salesperson.

The intercom buzzes, interrupting my rambling thoughts. I practically sprint the eight feet to press the Talk button on the wall next to the door.

"I'll be right down," I shout (I always shout, I can't help it).

No way do I want Tobias in my tiny apartment—yet. I'm not ashamed of it, but... we'd be alone, and... I shake my head as I slide my feet into my leather loafers. I can't think about being alone with him; my brain will explode. Making sure I have my wallet and phone, I lock up behind myself and race down the stairs. I never take the elevator if I don't have to.

Outside, Tobias is waiting for me behind the wheel of a shiny black Audi Q7. I open the passenger door and slide into the seat.

"Hey. Thanks for driving," I say, ever so cleverly.

Tobias grins at me. Wow, his smile is seriously dangerous: the way his face lights up and the cute smile lines at the corner of his eyes. I smile back at him, ignoring the confusing little flutter in the region of my heart. That flutter is getting more insistent, and I'm close to admitting I have actual feelings for this sweet man.

There is massive traffic, and some streets are closed off due to the block party, forcing Tobias to take a circuitous detour along Lake Washington to I-5. Ten minutes into the drive I'm thinking it would have been better for us to have ridden the bus, even if the trip would've taken two extra hours.

The unfortunate truth is, Tobias Barrington is a terrible driver.

As surreptitiously as possible, I clutch the passenger door and make sure my seat belt is firmly anchored, ignoring Tobias's sideways glance at me as I do so.

Oh, the irony. Here I am, alone in a car with Tobias Barrington, and instead of being able to chat as we drive, Tobias channels a mix of Dale Earnhardt and my own mother that has me fearing for life and limb and unable to form complete sentences.

I'm absolutely certain Tobias learned to drive from the same clown who taught my mom. Stop signs are suggestions, Yield signs are slight hesitations, and unless there is an oncoming car, Tobias uses both lanes equally, straddling the center line.

Road construction that has been ongoing since before we were sparks in our parents' eyes (or a broken condom, if I can believe my father) has to be navigated along the way. Along the lake, some of the lanes are hardly wide enough for two cars. When we reach the intersection where drivers are supposed to enter the freeway, the traffic is always like something out of a Bourne movie. Complete chaos reigns. Cars change lanes willy-nilly. Right turns on red lights, illegal lefts, drivers who can't seem to find the stop line or understand what a crosswalk is— this area alone is why I don't drive anymore.

Tobias glances over at me again. "Nervous?"

"Um." How did one answer that? I'm terrified.

Tobias chuckles. "I don't drive very often."

He glances over at me again. I want to take his face in my hands and turn it forward, forcing him to keep his sexy eyes on the road.

"Oh, really?" My mouth is dry. Surely it would be bad form

to tell Tobias he's a terrible driver. This is our first fake date, even if all we're doing is going to what is bound to be an uncomfortable dinner with my mom and the skank dentist. I bite the inside of my lip.

"Are you worried about the dinner?" Tobias asks.

No, I'm worried about arriving to the dinner alive. When and if that happens, I'll start worrying about dinner. But at least I'm not stressing out about Tobias meeting my mom anymore.

As if he's reading my very thoughts, Tobias says, "Charley thinks I'm a terrible driver."

"Finally, something he and I agree on," I mutter.

"What?" Tobias asks.

"Nothing! I'm sure, um, with more practice you'll be an excellent driver." With great effort, I pry my fingers away from the passenger door handle and remind myself to take calming breaths. He hasn't actually hit anything. Yet.

"I'm a little nervous about dinner," I say instead. "Starting to think bringing you to meet my mother and the dentist was poorly thought out. What if I hate him? What if he's a complete jerk? What if he's bald and overweight and doesn't know how to eat with chopsticks?"

"Well…" Tobias glances over at me again.

"Eyes on the road," I snap, adding a sheepish, "please."

"Funny, that's what Charley says too."

Fucking Charley. Why do I have to agree with him about anything?

"Anyway," Tobias continues, "how long have they been dating? Has your mom ever introduced you to a boyfriend of hers before? And even if he is bald and overweight and doesn't know how to use chopsticks, if your mom likes him and he's nice to her, that's all that matters, right? It's what's inside that counts."

I sigh. God, here is Tobias Barrington being fucking perfect again. Because yes, he's right. All that matters is if Mom is happy with the dentist.

"I'm sorry I said that about him being fat and bald. Body shaming isn't cool. You're right, it doesn't matter." I sigh. At this rate I'm going to use up all the oxygen in the car. "I'm nervous."

"About you and me, or your mom?" I see Tobias glance in my direction again.

"Eyes on the road," I hiss. "Um..." I force myself to relax and slump down a little in my seat as I try to frame my answer while Tobias weaves through the Saturday evening freeway traffic. "My mom will love you. But what if this guy takes an instant dislike to me? I tend to say things without thinking... and I'm nervous, so I'm bound to say something awkward. This guy is probably Mister Perfect with his perfect daughters—did I mention he has two daughters?"

"Are they going to be there?"

"No, Mom promised it would just be the two of them. She wants me to meet him alone first. Probably because his kids are so perfect they outshine the sun," I say glumly.

"Maybe it's because your mom knows you'd feel over-whelmed otherwise? And I bet, from the little you've told me, that your mom thinks you are pretty awesome."

Tobias is so reasonable and right. Mom is 100 percent in my court. She's been my defender and supporter all my life. And, as nervous as I am, I know she'll do her best to keep this meet-the-dentist experience as stress-free as possible. I also know I don't want to let her down.

SIXTEEN

Chapter Sixteen—Tobias

THE RESTAURANT IS ABOUT HALF-FULL. Arnie and I pause at the hostess station for a second, and he's scanning the room for his mother when we hear a cheery, "Arnie! Over here!"

"Here we go. Are you ready?"

Arnie makes a face I *think* is supposed to be a game face. I have to suppress a snort of laughter. Arnie is acting as if we're headed into battle instead of dinner. I've participated in so many stilted, uncomfortable dinners, there's no way this could be worse. And if by some chance it is, we have plans for drinks afterward and we can both drown our sorrows.

Rita Ferguson is petite, with short dark hair and a mischievous smile. She looks just like her son—or rather, Arnie looks like his mother. She is a smaller, older version but very obviously related to my date.

"I forgot to warn you about the hugging," Arnie says out the side of his mouth as Rita rises from her chair, her arms open wide.

"And who's this?" she asks after squeezing the life out of Arnie.

"Mom, this is Tobias Barrington. Tobias, my mom, the one and only Rita Ferguson."

"Oh, darling, come here, let me hug you. Barrington? That's not a common name around here. You have to be Andrew's son. I knew him in college. Call me Rita." She squeezes me tightly as well, without giving me a chance to answer.

I remember now Arnie mentioning that the other night. "It's lovely to meet you," I say.

"Mom, be nice," Arnie hisses.

Rita winks at me, then turns and gestures toward the very ordinary-looking middle-aged man who'd also stood up from his seat when we arrived.

"Arnie, Tobias, this is Will Bordon. Will, darling, you finally get to meet my son, Arnie."

I notice Arnie twitch at her use of the word "darling," but he politely shakes the other man's hand before sitting down.

Will Bordon isn't bald. He has a head full of dark hair sprinkled with sparks of silver here and there. He's heavyset, and while he's not as tall as me, he is taller than Arnie. He smiles at us with kind eyes before shaking my hand too.

Arnie and I are sitting on one side of the table, Rita and Will on the other. The waiter immediately comes over; do we want drinks before we order our dinner? Arnie stares at the menu, scanning the choices, while I order an Arnold Palmer. I don't drive very often, and driving all the way back to Madison after having a few drinks is a bad idea. I didn't miss Arnie holding on to the passenger door like he was on the sinking *Titanic* and it was the door that would save him.

The waiter departs with our orders, and I turn my attention to Rita and Will. Rita has a million questions; I can tell from the curious expression on her face. Just like her son, she doesn't hide her emotions well—or at all.

"This is a surprise, Arnie, a pleasant one. How did you and Tobias meet?" The table wobbles, and Rita frowns, whatever she'd been about to say next going unsaid.

"Work—yes, Tobias comes into the Buzz, where I work," Arnie gabbles. "We had a da—a plan to go to the block party tonight. But, you know, dinner with you is always great. And Tobias wanted to meet you too. A mother-son moment. We're both getting the awkward meet-the-boyfriend thing taken care of at the same time."

Arnie shuts his mouth with a snap, seeming to rewind what he's said and blushing a fiery red. He grabs his glass of ice water and chugs it down. I like that he used the word "boyfriend," but I think if I say anything he might spontaneously combust.

The waiter reappears with our drinks. Arnie sets his water down so he can take a big sip of his cocktail.

"Oh, the block party—those were the days of my youth," Rita says into the silence.

The conversation turns to what about Seattle has and hasn't changed since Rita's youth. I find myself liking Arnie's mom. It's obvious she adores Arnie and wants him to be happy —and she also wants Arnie to like Will Bordon. Having her son meet Will is a big deal. I wonder if they're more serious than Arnie realizes... and what Arnie will think about it when he finds out.

AN HOUR and two mojitos later, Arnie has relaxed and is torturing me with a sweet and sour shrimp clamped securely between his chopsticks as he waves it around. "These are my absolute favorite." He rolls his eyes, making a ridiculous face. I can't help but laugh, watching as Arnie pops the shrimp into his mouth. When his tongue sneaks out to lick his lips, I shift in my seat.

I'm fascinated by Arnie's lips, wet from licking them clean. I want to do something totally absurd—I want to lean over and kiss him right there in the middle of the restaurant. I want to taste the sweet and sour directly from his lips. I force myself to look away and catch Rita watching me with a thoughtful expression.

"So, you don't really remind me much of your father," Rita comments.

"Mom!" Arnie looks horrified.

I nudge Arnie with my elbow. "That's probably a good thing."

"We were at the U at the same time. Didn't always see eye to eye. Your dad is one of those people. I'm sorry; he just rubbed me the wrong way."

Arnie opens his mouth, to say *what* I have no idea, but I get there first. I also know who Arnie inherited his honesty from.

"Let me guess," I say, smiling. "You were all 'Save the whales,' and he was more 'Why have old buildings when we can tear them down and build new ones?' I can assure you he hasn't changed much."

Rita nods her agreement. "And I still am all about the whales. Tell me about yourself, Tobias."

I find myself sharing with Rita and Will my dream of someday writing screenplays. How movies have always fascinated me and I've been interested ever since I was small in how they're made, from beginning to end. Unlike what I think will be my father's reaction, they are kind and ask lots of questions.

"Do you think you'll move to LA someday?" Will asks.

"I can't see myself living there. I've visited plenty of times, and I don't think I'd like it much."

All in all, dinner isn't the disaster Arnie predicted it would be. I'm fairly certain he enjoyed himself. Will makes a big effort to engage with him, although there's another time the table inexplicably rocks when Will asks Arnie about his degree in data science. I lean down and check underneath it to see if we need to jam a coaster or a wad of napkins under one leg, but it seems steady enough.

Instead, Arnie goes on a tirade about the use of Latin in movies and TV shows, obviously a topic close to his heart. His hands are flying everywhere as he tries to describe how irritating it is to have bad Latin. And, secondarily, that demons (I'm not sure what they have to do with anything) wouldn't speak Latin anyway—they presumably existed long before Latin and would have a language of their own, he argues. Why would using Latin spells allow a person to summon a demon?

Will-the-dentist manages to hold his own, and by the time we're all getting ready to go, I'm pretty sure Arnie doesn't hate him. And Will adores Rita, that much is evident to me.

"Darling son, thank you for spending a Saturday evening with your old mom. And it was lovely to meet you as well, Tobias. We'll have to do this again soon." She hugs us both before waving and heading across the lot to where she and Will parked. Arnie follows them, hugging his mom one more time before she gets in her car.

Unlocking the doors of my car, I climb inside. It's stuffy and hot from sitting in the sun, so I start it and get the AC going. When Arnie gets in, he slumps dramatically into the passenger seat with his forearm covering his eyes and groans. I can't help but chuckle.

"We survived, and I managed not to call him the skank boyfriend. I deserve a medal." He rolls his head in my direction. "And I need another drink. Let's stop at the Blue?"

"Sure." I'm not ready for the evening to end. It's still pretty early.

The drive back to Leschi is much quieter than the drive out. I wonder what Arnie is thinking about, but at least he's not stressing out about my driving.

Arnie finally breaks the silence. "I think she likes him."

"Well…" I choose my words carefully. As much as I have to learn about Arnie, one thing I already know is he's sensitive and a little bit possessive of Rita. "I got that impression too. He seems like a nice guy; I think he likes her a lot."

"Ugh. I think I like him too."

"That's good, right?"

"Yes, it's good. I was all ready to hate his pants off. But Will is nothing like my bio father—thankfully. You know," he says thoughtfully, "I've never actually been able to figure that out."

"Figure what out?"

"How my mom and dad got together and, when they did, why they stayed together for so long. They're complete opposites. I'm not saying my mom is perfect or anything—after all, she did agree to dye my hair green once, and even though it was a disaster, I still love her—but my dad is a complete asshole. You should've seen my hair. Instead of looking like a punk rocker, I looked like a mutant dandelion. The dye didn't take right, and my hair turned this odd shade of yellow. It was super brittle too and would just break off."

"A dandelion? How old were you—when was this?" I chuckle, imagining Arnie with a yellow-green plume of hair floating around his head.

"Oh," Arnie says airily, "a freshman in high school. My reputation, such as it was, never recovered."

I can so relate to Arnie's feelings about his dad, but I don't want to talk about my own dad right now. I don't want to poison the atmosphere by mentioning his name; it was bad enough when Rita brought up knowing him.

"Maybe there was something between your folks in the beginning, but it wasn't sustainable or something?"

"I guess." Arnie sounds skeptical. "Probably Mom was swept off her feet, and by the time she realized he was complete tool, it was too late."

I navigate a curve in the boulevard, and the neon sign for the Blue appears in the distance. Slowing to a stop, I wait for an oncoming car to pass by before turning left into the parking lot.

As we walk toward the entrance, Arnie pulls his phone from his pocket and frowns at it, stopping by another parked car.

"Something wrong?" My cell phone has vibrated in my pocket a few times, but after glancing at it I'd tucked it away. Charley could wait.

"It's Gale, from work. Some kind of emergency, she needs me to open tomorrow. Dang it." Arnie huffs and shoves his phone back into his pocket. "I should go home. Four a.m. is going to come awfully fast."

"Cinderfella has to be home before midnight?" I tease.

Arnie scowls. "Yes, Cinderfella doesn't like to lose his beauty sleep." His voice turns soft. "I was looking forward to having a drink."

Somehow, I sense Arnie is blushing when he admits that, and I wish the light in the parking lot were brighter so I'd know for sure.

"Me too. Rain check? We can maybe try again next week?"

I have a busy week ahead; my dad is still insisting on hiring an office assistant. I'd protested, but on Friday, Carly, my dad's personal assistant, stopped me on the way out to tell me interviews had already happened and a new person is starting sometime next week.

Arnie glances up at me, a complicated and tentative smile hovering on his lips. "Okay, next week. I'll text you?"

I don't want to wait until next week. I want to lean in and

kiss him, but something holds me back. When it happens, I want it to be perfect. I want it to be romantic and spontaneous.

Arnie is funny. He makes me laugh—in a good way. His honesty is refreshing. I'm tired of people agreeing with me because they think they have to (my coworkers), and I hate trying to guess what someone is really thinking. In some ways, Arnie is a lot like Charley—even though I'm pretty sure both of them will deny any similarity between them to their dying days.

All those years ago I'd been captivated by Arnie, and recognizing him at the coffee shop had revived my nascent feelings as if it been days, not years, since I'd last seen him.

"Can I give you a ride home?" I offer.

Arnie is... intricate, like one of those Chinese puzzle boxes my dad collects and keeps in his study. You might accidentally unlock one part of it, but the rest remains a secret: you have to open the drawers in the right order to find the real treasure. I want to be the one who figures him out. I want to know the real Arnie Ferguson.

"No," he replies, "it's literally three blocks from here. I think I need the walk, and I'm pretty sure if you come along, I won't be getting to bed anytime soon. I mean, not that I assume anything would happen—or not happen—what I mean is, I'm kind of grouchy when I don't get enough sleep. Kill me now." He's looking at me, his eyes wide behind his glasses.

I laugh, because he's right—something would happen, I'm pretty sure. "I had a great night. Your mom is awesome, and her new guy seemed nice too."

Arnie looks down, scuffing the pavement with his loafer. "Yeah, he didn't scream serial killer, I suppose." He glances back up at me, his eyes narrowing. "Did you notice how she never said exactly how they met? I'm going to have to ignore the fact that my mother probably has a profile on a dating site. I just can't know that kind of thing."

I snicker. "Luckily you aren't in the same demographic—I mean, if you had a dating profile yourself, you wouldn't find your mom's."

Arnie's eyes widen comically. "No. No, I can't even... Can you imagine? I'd literally die. On the spot. I do not want to know what my mother listed as her interests. Dentists? Maybe that was a hobby. I really need to head home now."

He doesn't move right away, fidgeting a bit before glancing back at me one last time and then turning to head up the hill toward his apartment building.

I want to run after him and kiss him, but my feet won't move. I should've done it instead of overthinking it. I reassure myself there will be another opportunity. I want to kiss him, dammit, and I should've taken the chance.

"SPILL," Charley demands. Not ready to go home yet, I called him from the Blue's parking lot, thinking he would still be out at the block party with Duff Cleveland; whatever that was about.

"Why were you texting me? I was *on a date*. I know it might be something you've never done, but it's a traditional way two people get to know each other."

"Are you at home?"

"At the Blue. Arnie and I were going to grab a drink before I took him home, but he got called to work in the morning."

"You drove?" Charley laughs evilly. "No wonder he ran off. I'll grab a Lyft and be there in ten minutes. Don't start drinking without me."

I'm lucky to grab two spots at the bar, sliding in as a couple leaves and snagging the empty stool with my foot. The Blue is hopping at this time of night. There's a diverse crowd, one I feel comfortable among. While I'm waiting for Charley to arrive, I order a beer.

I'm about halfway through it when Charley slides onto the seat next to me.

Charley points at my beer. "That looks like a drink to me."

I lift one shoulder. "I wasn't just going to just sit here."

The bartender stops in front of us, and Charley orders a Manhattan.

"Why aren't you still at the block party?" I ask him.

"Let's not talk about me. I want to hear about meeting the parents."

"What happened?" I know something happened, or Charley wouldn't have texted

Charley's drink lands in front of him, and he takes a long swallow, his eyes flickering shut in enjoyment. "I'm getting drunk. I ran into Simon."

Ah. Simon Ellison, Charley's ex.

"I thought he was overseas, research or something."

Charley sips his drink again. "I did too. At least, that's the last I'd heard." His tone has a finality to it that means, tonight at least, we won't be discussing Simon Ellison any further.

"How bad was it?"

"I panicked and kissed this guy I was dancing with. The dancing was fine, but it was like kissing a board."

I giggle, immediately biting my lips closed at the murderous expression on Charley's face.

"Then what happened, and... why?" I ask. Obviously something happened, or Charley wouldn't be chugging his Manhattan.

Charley ignores the *why* part of my question, but I'm pretty sure the only thing that would make him kiss a stranger is seeing his ex. "He made me promise to 'never try anything like that again.'" He shudders. "It was terrible. To make matters worse, after a few excruciating moments of pretending we both weren't completely horrified, Eli spotted a guy he claimed to know and basically dumped me."

I barely resist pointing out that he and the dancing guy had never been together. The bartender comes back, and Charley orders another drink. "And the same for my friend here." He gestures at me with his thumb. "Anyway, I'm not here about me. I'm here in my official capacity as your best friend."

I tell him everything, even about wanting to kiss Arnie but not doing it. Also that we have a tentative date for next week.

"Huh. Sounds nice, and almost normal."

"It was fun. Arnie's mom is really nice. She made a comment about me being 'Andrew's son,' but that was it. I mean, Andrew's managed to step on a lot of toes over the years. I'm not surprised she's a member of his anti-fan club."

"Huh."

"That's all? 'Huh'?"

Charley shrugs again. "Knowing your dad, he either tried to get in her pants or tried to get her to invest in some scheme of his."

I nod in agreement and glumly take a sip of my Manhattan. "Or both."

"Or both," Charley agrees.

Then, seeing as Charley has a third Manhattan—running into Simon always depresses him, even if he denies it—I give him a ride home, with him complaining about my driving the entire way.

Chapter Seventeen—Arnie

I STUMBLE up the hill to my apartment building. It's still warm out, and the sun is setting, but I don't pay attention to the show tonight. My brain is churning a million miles an hour—a kaleidoscope of thoughts, and none I'm able to focus properly on; they twirl and float just out of my reach.

Tobias, dinner, Will, my mom. Tobias laughing as Mom told a story about when I tried out for Pee Wee football—spoiler alert, I didn't make the team—all mixed with the drinks and delicious food. The job interview. The job interview I haven't told Tobias about yet. Yet. The fact that I think I like Will. I want to hate him, but seeing my mom laugh and lean into him made all the difference. I'm not excited to meet his kids, but I know it's coming.

With all these feelings swirling around, I'm not paying as much attention as maybe I should be when I let myself into the studio.

Lost in my very confusing and distracting thoughts, I push the door open and flick the overhead light on at the same time. At first I don't know what I'm seeing, until my eyes move from the stranger's face full of cock upward and I recognize Duff's shocked expression. And then I'm wishing I hadn't; I'm wishing there really was something like eye bleach or brain bleach, because I'm *never* going to be able to erase this from my mind.

"Jesus Christ, Duff!" I shriek, loudly enough our neighbors can probably hear me over their TV shows.

Scrabbling backward along the wall with my eyes squeezed shut, I slam the light back off so I can't see my roommate's dick in someone else's mouth. Not that I want it in my—no, no, no, no, I can't even go there—I just have no desire to see Duff's, or some stranger's, junk.

Even with the lights off, it's never truly dark in our studio. I can still see Duff and blow-job guy, so I sidle into the kitchenette and turn my back to the spectacle.

"What the ever-loving fucking hell... have... have you never heard of putting a sock on the door? Even me, no-sex Arnie, has heard of that. What the hell?" I sputter as I open the refrigerator door and pretend to look for something inside.

"Arnie?"

"Seriously, Duff, what the fuck?" I say to the mayonnaise.

"Arnie!"

"What?"

Duff says, with what I think is ill-placed impatience, "Would you please shut the front door? I'm sure we don't need any of the neighbors over here."

Huffing, I edge across the small space and close the door. As much as I want to slam it, I manage to shut it quietly.

When I turn my attention back to my roommate, Duff, *thankfully*, is pulling his pants back up, and the other guy—as usual, no one I've met before—is also straightening his clothes.

"I can't even—" I shake my head, belatedly realizing the other guy is not Charley, with whom Duff supposedly has been on a date. This guy is toned and muscly. The tight-fitting tank top and running pants he wears display his tree-trunk arms and massive thighs—at least twenty-five inches.

I flick the light back on, making all of us blink.

"What about yoga guy? What happened to him?" I ask.

"Yoga guy? Who's that?" blow-job guy asks. He has a nice voice, deep and rumbly—or maybe that's from having Duff's cock jammed down his throat.

Duff rolls his eyes. "Nobody," he says.

"Ohhh," blow-job guy says, nodding as if he and Duff have a secret.

"Introduce me," I say.

"What?" asks Duff.

"Introduce me to your new friend"—I gesture toward muscle man—"so I can stop referring to him as blow-job guy in my head."

Duff smirks. "Arnie, this is Devon. Devon, this is my roommate and best friend, Arnie."

"Sorry, I'm not shaking your hand," I say to Devon, "but nice to meet you."

DUFF ISN'T NEARLY CONTRITE ENOUGH, in my opinion. Once Devon leaves—and he didn't seem embarrassed at being interrupted, either; am I the only gay man in Seattle who's not an exhibitionist? I like sex, but when I have it (rarely), I like it to be between me and my partner, not the entire city.

"So, what happened on *your* date tonight?" Duff asks after locking the door behind Devon.

I open one of our windows and turn on the desk fan to try to entice even the tiniest breeze inside. "It wasn't a date. It was dinner with my mother so she could introduce me to her new boyfriend."

"A dinner you invited Tobias Barrington along on. Therefore, date. Oh, a double date with your mother."

I decide to ignore Duff's comment. "Dinner was fine."

"And how was the new boyfriend—your mother's, just to clarify."

Turning from fiddling with the fan, I try to laser Duff with my glare. It doesn't work. Duff just chuckles, crosses to the closet, and opens it, rummaging around in his section.

"He seems okay," I allow. "Nice enough. I'm pretty sure he has designs on Mom."

"Designs? What decade are you living in?"

"One where I don't want to think about my mom having sex, okay? I don't think that's particularly weird."

"Yeah, I suppose you're right."

Duff's voice is muffled as he pulls off the T-shirt he's wearing and tosses it aside. He tugs a fresh one over his head before heading to his futon to lie down with his arms behind his head.

I undress carefully, putting my new clothes away and pulling a T-shirt and sleep pants on before lying down to stare at the ceiling myself. It's mostly dark in the studio, but I've stared above my bed enough over the past couple of years that I have the ceiling memorized. I don't need to see the intricate cracks in order to trace them with my eyes.

"I had fun," I finally say. "I liked him. And Tobias was perfect."

Duff says quietly, "You sound surprised."

I think about it. "I was, am, surprised."

Tobias is nice, and funny, and listens to me when I ramble.

I'm not going to admit anything more to Duff. I don't need

Duff crowing about how he's been right all along and I do actually have feelings for Tobias.

Are we... dating now? We haven't even kissed. But I accidentally called him my boyfriend, and I took him to dinner with my mother as if we were really dating. And afterward, in the parking lot of the Blue, it had felt like the end of a real date to me, when I hadn't meant it to. I want to kiss Tobias; Jesus, I want to climb him like a tree. Kissing Tobias would not make me want to gag. Kissing Tobias would be epic—and I'm pretty sure Tobias wants to kiss me too.

Boyfriends are supposed to want to kiss each other. But we aren't boyfriends (because: *revenge*), and I have no intention of allowing my heart to get involved, right? Except my heart seems to have other ideas.

This is all about karma. Karma, karma, karma.

If you say it enough times, it makes it true. Right?

The sneaky little voice in my head is not sure.

Arnie Sedgewick Ferguson, I admonish myself, what have you done? I squeeze my eyes shut and admit to myself what happened earlier, and I silently groan.

I *maybe* went on a real date, that's what I did.

I'm attached already.

I'm a complete fool.

Flopping over again, I kick my thin blanket off my body. The faintest breeze is creeping in through the open window, and I lift up my T-shirt, flapping it to get the most of it. The breeze doesn't help cool me down.

Isn't this exactly what I want? I need to stay focused on the goal: righting the wrong, balancing the karma. I can't let myself get wrapped up in the fact that Tobias is a really nice guy and seems to like me right back. Which is weird in itself, because most guys think I'm too much work.

"There's nothing going on between me and Tobias."

Because there couldn't be.

"Whatever you wanna think," replies Duff, his voice sleepy.

I lie awake for a long time thinking I'm fooling myself about my feelings for Tobias.

EIGHTEEN

Chapter Eighteen—Tobias

SUNDAY IS the one day of the week the Barrington household is left to its own devices. Our chef has the day off, as well as my dad's personal assistant and the groundskeepers. I have a habit of taking my laptop out to the greenhouse to work on ideas for screenplays. My one idea, anyway.

The class I'm taking focuses on comedy writing. I don't think I'm very good at comedy writing. It requires a sort of faultless banter I can't seem to manage—not easily anyway. I'm more interested in art house movie writing; I have an idea for a screenplay about a gay used-car salesman in a turf battle with the owners of a new lot that opens up across the street run by a macho straight guy—something along the lines of *Repo Man*. It will be a long time, though, before I feel comfortable showing an outline to anyone.

The garden structure isn't an actual greenhouse; it's a glass building that at some point in time was wired for electricity. Olivia likes to hold brunches and society meetings here. I've attended innumerable tea parties hosted by my sister. The other guests were usually an overstuffed teddy bear, a doll wearing clothing that cost nearly as much as my own, and a cowgirl doll complete with boots, jeans, a plaid shirt, and a wide-brimmed hat. The cowgirl was always the guest of honor.

Picking up my laptop, I leave my bedroom and take the back stairs two at a time to the ground floor. The stairs lead first to the kitchen and then to a side door to the back garden. In the kitchen, I stop and fill a mug with coffee. Our cook always leaves the coffee pot prepped and on a timer. She probably thinks my parents have no idea how to manage such a thing and is likely right.

With coffee in one hand and my laptop under my arm, I open the side door and ease outside. If I'm lucky, I'll be able to work for a few hours before anyone except Sarah-Michelle thinks to look for me.

"HEY, big brother, I thought I'd find you out here."

I glance up at the sound of my sister's voice; I'd been so engrossed in my imaginary world I hadn't heard her approach.

"Hey, kid."

Sarah-Michelle cocks one hip and raises an elegant eyebrow. "Not a kid."

"You'll always be my kid sister."

She huffs. Her bangs float upward for a moment as she pulls out the matching wicker chair and flops down in it. "How's the writing going?"

I raise my eyebrows at her. Two can play this game.

"Obviously, before I interrupted you."

"Good, I think," I answer, sitting back in my seat.

"Rowan told me you had a date last night."

This is the thing about Sarah-Michelle: as different as she is from our father—as in, she is caring, empathetic, and self-aware —she is also direct, ambitious, and focused, like him. She has a mind like a steel trap. If Charley's younger sister even hinted about something like me being on a date, Sarah-Michelle won't have missed it.

"I thought you and Rowan didn't hang out much anymore."

Sarah-Michelle flips her long dark hair back over her shoulder, piercing me with a knowing look. "She's on the authorized list of people I'm allowed to associate with. I go over to her house, and we cover for each other. She's not terrible, just not terribly interesting. Anyway, about your date."

"Maybe you should consider the FBI as a career. Or Special Forces—they could probably use an interrogator like you," I grumble.

"Look, big brother, if I'm going be backing you up, I need to know all the details."

"It wasn't a date."

She eyes me again. "You took your car out."

I sigh. "Arnie needed a wingman. He was meeting his mom's new boyfriend."

"Huh. That's not what drunk Charley told Rowan."

I should've known better than to drop Charley off before he'd sobered up a bit. Rowan must've been lying in wait.

"Fine. Arnie Ferguson. He works at the Buzz."

Sarah-Michelle's green-brown gaze bores into me.

"Fine," I repeat. "I met him a few years ago. We met at, uh, a party."

Sarah-Michelle's eyes widen. "Ohhh, this wouldn't be the party you had here when Mom dragged me off to that awful mother-daughter yoga retreat in Costa Rica and Dad had a business meeting in Zurich?"

I blink, trying, and failing, to come up with a reason why *the party* would pop into Sarah-Michelle's mind.

"Why, of all the parties I've ever been to, would you think it was that one?"

"Tobias, that party was scandalous! You're never scandalous, and the one time you were, you went big and the police got called. Mom actually had to take a call *during* yoga. Do you think she hasn't mentioned it ten or one hundred times over the past few years? Not that I'm bitter or anything, but that party meant I've been under the spotlight for years in case I might also become a deviant." She looks thoughtful for a moment, then adds, "It might not have been so bad if there had been one or two token girls, but with only guys..."

"There was..." At least one girl? I think. Never mind. "Mom and Dad," I start to protest, "aren't homo—"

Sarah-Michelle raises one hand, stopping my words. "Mom wants to keep living in her little bubble of happiness, and you being gay isn't an issue as long as she never has to think about it. Dad... he's never said anything, but I think he knows better, in a town like Seattle, than to be a vocal homophobe. Look around the office, though: how many people other than yourself are out?"

I have looked around in the couple of years I've been at Barrington, and I don't know anyone else who's out.

"What does this have to do with me going, or not going, on a date?"

"If you bring home a boyfriend, it's going to make it real."

"Charley's gay. He's here all the time."

"Yes, but Charley and Rowan's parents have more money than Mom and Dad. They're old-school Seattle society. Rowan's mom never had to apply for club memberships; they were already members."

"I still don't see how my boyfriend would matter in all this."

"Yes, you do. Especially if he"—Sarah-Michelle raises both hands and makes quote marks with her fingers—"isn't rich enough. And I have the feeling that if he works at a coffee shop, he isn't rich enough for Dad."

This is a fear that has been hanging around in the back of my mind. Sarah-Michelle is right: our parents are the worst snobs. They'll take one look at Arnie Ferguson and do everything they can to get rid of him.

Sarah-Michelle leans forward, her expression serious. "You need to move out. I know why you've stayed, and thank you. I can handle the 'rents myself now, but if I do need you, I know how to get a hold of you."

Moving out is something I want—badly—but it's seemed easier and smarter to live in my parents' house to support Sarah-Michelle.

"I would've been okay anyway, you know, but thank you for being here."

"Are you... kicking me out of the nest?" I ask, grinning at my sister while mentally tallying my savings and the number of months (eight, it's only been a few days since I last counted) until my twenty-fifth birthday.

"Yes. It's my senior year, and I want to enjoy it without worrying about you."

"What? Why would you worry about me?"

"Tobias, I may be seventeen, but I'm not stupid. I know why you're still here, and I worry that it keeps you from being happy."

"Well, I'm twenty-four and not as smart as you."

"When do I get to meet him?"

I almost ask, *meet who.* "Uh, it's early days."

Never mind the fact that I agreed to tag along the first time Arnie met his mom's new boyfriend, I have the distinct impression he would run for the hills if I suggested he meet my family. Plus, Arnie is mine. I'm not sure I want my parents meeting him and passing judgment. And they would pass judgment. For Andrew it's practically an Olympic sport.

"You like him, though?"

I nod, smiling. "I do, he's..." How to describe Arnie Ferguson? "He's very smart, even though he works at a coffee shop. He's funny, although I think it's by accident most of the time. I think he doesn't have a great brain-to-mouth filter. He just says what he's thinking. He says I'm a terrible driver."

"You *are* a terrible driver."

I shrug. "I can't be perfect in all ways."

NINETEEN

Chapter Nineteen—Arnie

"WELL?" Gale corners me in the dish pit during a lull between customers. Sundays are a little different, as we open later and customers stay longer, enjoying the Buzz's modified brunch menu and homemade pastries.

"Well, what?" I'm going to try to play this cool; I don't owe Gale any information.

Oh, wait, I totally owe her, even if Duff and Charley seem to have opposite-magnetism. Is that a thing? It must be.

"How did your date go?" Gale cocks her head, fingers in her pockets as she leans against one wall, watching me.

Ugh, now I realize I neglected to tell her about the circumstances during the week that led to Tobias meeting my mom instead of us having fun at the block party. And the fact that I called off the whole Duff and Charley shenanigans. I'm not very good at sticking to a plan.

I grab one of the gray bus tubs, balance it on the counter, and begin to empty the plates into the dishwasher.

"Was it that bad?"

"No!" I say hastily. "It was fine. Fun, even." The bottom rack filled, I push it back in and pull out the top one. I load the ceramic cups and water glasses while thinking about what to tell Gale.

After pushing the door shut and pressing the start button, I turn around and lean against the stainless steel sink, mimicking Gale's pose. The dishwasher starts up noisily behind me.

"I ended up having to go to dinner with my mom instead of the block party. She wanted me to meet her new boyfriend. Tobias, uh, went with me."

There's a far-too-short silence before Gale opens her mouth. "You took Tobias with you to meet your mom and her new BF? How'd that go?"

I can't tell if Gale thinks I've been smart or foolish.

"Tobias charmed my mom and the boyfriend."

"What did *you* think about your mom's new boyfriend?"

I hate it when Gale manages to get to the heart of my worries. She knows me far too well.

"He seemed fine. Okay, he wasn't that bad. Probably not a serial killer, but I haven't had time to stalk him online. My mom really likes him. He's a dentist." I spit out the word "dentist" as if it's the most heinous career choice a person could make. Just going to the dentist skeeves me. I shudder convulsively.

Gale chuckles. "Last I heard, being a dentist wasn't a war crime."

"I know," I grunt. The last person I want to think about right now is my mom's new boyfriend. I know how lucky I am; my mom has always been there for me. I'm happy for her. I honest-to-god am. It's just a lot to take in.

I don't know for certain, but I suspect one factor in my parents' divorce had been *me*. Where my mother supports me, my father sees nothing but failure and certainly not the son he wanted, a mirror image of himself.

"They both liked Tobias."

"What about you?" Gale asks.

"Maybe I'm not cut out for this revenge stuff," I mutter.

"Maybe it's because you like him too," Gale says wisely.

Probably.

Okay, fine, yes. I do really like Tobias. I'm like a middle schooler with my first crush. Gah, seven years ago I kissed Tobias when I was drunk and imprinted on him like a baby duckling. How foolish am I? And how foolish am I not to realize it before now?

"If I admit it, will you leave me alone?"

Grinning, Gale stands away from the wall, ready to head back out to the dining area. "Sure."

I don't believe her.

I ALSO DON'T BELIEVE the Barrington HR representative when she calls Monday morning.

"Mr. Ferguson, we'd like to offer you the position."

I'd thought the in-person interview went okay, but still, I'm shocked. I should be jumping up and down with joy, but instead my stomach suddenly feels like it's filled with lead, and I pause too long before saying anything. I never told Tobias about applying at Barrington Properties, and now it seems weird and wrong of me.

"Wow, that's, uh, amazing," I manage weakly.

I'm planning on declining the offer, until she quotes me a starting salary that is a third more than Gale can pay me, plus a lot of detail about health benefits and vacation time that I don't really hear. "If that's satisfactory, we'd like to get you going with the onboarding process."

My start date is set for next week. "We like to have new hires start midweek; it's not as overwhelming," the woman says. I know Gale won't mind if I don't give a full two-week notice.

I hang up feeling like I might vomit. I'm torn between elation at landing a new, better-paying job and the fact that I'm going to have to tell Tobias.

This is what I want, right? Why am I not happier? I wish Duff were home to talk to, but he's at some in-city yoga retreat, or maybe he has a photo gig. Who knows? He just as easily could've road-tripped to Sedona to reinvigorate his chakra, or whatever. At the moment, Sedona sounds good to me: nice and far from Seattle.

My mom will be over the moon about the job—she bought me an entire wardrobe, after all. But I don't want to tell her yet. I need to figure things out first.

I like Tobias. *Like*, like. As Gale so helpfully pointed out.

Liking complicates everything. I'm not supposed to like Tobias. I'm supposed to hate him and want to wreak my heady revenge. The universe is playing tricks on me. Instead of me getting revenge and thus getting my life on track, it's more messed up than it was before. But with a better salary.

HOWEVER, it isn't until Tobias texts me that evening that I understand how much trouble I'm actually in.

The Buzz is slow, and I'm hanging out behind the counter counting down the minutes before I can turn off the neon Open sign and go home.

Tobias: Hi

Arnie: Hi

Tobias: I have a busy week, how about Friday after work?

Technically I don't have any free time, because I'm working

as many shifts as I can before my last day. I stare at my phone trying to get my brain to work, wanting the right, witty reply to float to the top of my head like the responses in a Magic 8-Ball. I don't know how to tell Tobias I've accepted a job at his dad's company.

Arnie: I close a lot this week, Friday is one of those shifts.

Tobias: What about tomorrow?

Arnie: After 8, but I could try and get off earlier, maybe 7?

It suddenly seems very important I convince Eli to swap shifts with me. Eli owes me a favor or two. Surely he can do the last cleanup and let me leave at seven.

Tobias: Plenty of time for a movie!

Arnie: What movie?

Tobias: What movie do you want to see? Do you like big Hollywood movies or indies?

I hardly ever go to the movies. For one thing, they're expensive, and for another I have a thing about audience noise. Why do people pay twenty-five dollars (or more!) for a movie and snacks to talk, rustle, scratch, crinkle, and generally annoy me right at the most important plot point? Duff dragged me to the opening of the latest Captain America movie, and I nearly murdered the couple sitting in front of us because they *would not quit whispering.*

Tobias: There's a Jim Jarmusch retrospective at the Egyptian this week.

Who's Jim Jarmusch? I copy the name so I can look him up later.

Tobias: We could go watch a weird and wonderful movie and then head up Broadway for a late dinner or drinks?

Damn, the man can text fast.

Arnie: Okay.

Tobias: We can decide where to meet later, I gotta go.

I spend the few minutes until closing reading about the film-maker Jim Jarmusch; I spend the rest of the night worrying about the new job.

On the one hand, I'm excited. The pay is a big improvement, and the work seems like it could be something I'd enjoy. Maybe if Duff is able to get his financial crap worked out, we'll be able to afford a bigger apartment with two bedrooms, so I never walk in on him having sex again. That would just be one of the perks.

If things work out with Tobias...

I shut my eyes, blocking out the cracks in the ceiling and trying to also block out what is becoming more and more obvious, even to me: I want things to work out with Tobias. What started out as a plan for evening the score between us has turned into me having *feelings* for him.

The job at Barrington Properties is either going to be fantastic or I'm going to fantastically fail. My stomach projects failure. My heart hopes for something else.

And I still don't know how to tell Tobias about what I've done.

TWENTY

Chapter Twenty—Tobias

"WHERE ARE YOU GOING?" my dad calls when I walk past his office door on my way out.

There are a lot of answers I could give, but I choose to be honest—because I know it will set Andrew off, and because I refuse to apologize for it.

"I have a date."

"You don't have time to date. You have work to do. That presentation for the monthly meeting had better be finished."

I don't bother to respond. I hear my dad get up from his creaky office chair, but I don't stop walking. My sister is right, beyond right. I need to escape Barrington Properties. I haven't been doing myself any kind of favors by letting my father bully me into the only degree he would pay for—and then expect me to work here. I should've just taken loans out, knowing I would have the money to pay them back when I turned twenty-five.

And even if I am busy with meetings and networking events

I'm supposed to be preparing for and attending, I didn't want to wait a whole week before seeing Arnie again. I just couldn't. I begged, bribing Carly with iced coffees to help me out with the preparation for the various meetings so I could leave early today.

Maybe I'm overthinking things (this is very likely), but I feel like I need to act fast. Something about Arnie is tenuous and slippery, like he might disappear from my life at any moment. It's taken me since the summer before my senior year in high school to find him again, and I'm not letting him go easily.

Outside the building I pause for a second, checking for traffic before jogging across the street to where my car is parked. By seven I'm waiting outside the Buzz for Arnie, ignoring the butterflies acting like buffalo in my stomach.

I've only been waiting a few minutes, leaning against the fender of my car and watching the coffee shop door, when Arnie emerges looking a bit flustered. He spots me across the street and crosses over. I can't help but admire him. Sure, he's not gorgeous the way Charley is. No one would ever call Arnie a model. But he has a spark, a light about him that draws me. Maybe it's his wide mouth and ridiculous sense of humor, or his fierce glare when he's irritated; maybe it's the way his greenish-hazelish eyes seem to change color with his moods. I can't put my finger on what exactly it is about him. I only know I like it.

As Arnie gets closer, I realize that, if possible, Arnie is even more nervous and twitchy then Saturday, when we met Will-the-dentist. I am too; this time the date is real. I'm not merely a distraction.

"I'm not going to a movie wearing clothes that stink like coffee," Arnie declares.

I grin. "You look fine to me. But we can stop at your place if you want."

"I do want."

"Hop in."

Arnie hesitates; I can almost hear him thinking how terrible a driver I am.

"I promise I won't hit anything or run anyone over."

Arnie's eyes narrow, although I think I spy a glimmer of humor. "Hmmph" is all he says, but he gets into my car, which I count as a win, and moments later we're pulling over to the curb in front of Arnie's building.

"See, accident-free."

Arnie raises one eyebrow. "It was three blocks."

"Still, a lot could happen in three blocks!" I protest.

Arnie shakes his head. "I'll be right back."

I watch as he dashes to the front door and pulls it open. At the last second, he turns, catching my gaze. His lips curve into a shy smile, and he disappears inside. Making Arnie smile is my new favorite thing.

I PARK in my usual spot at home. There's no point in looking for parking along Broadway, and the theater isn't that far of a walk from here. It will be fun to mosey down the lively street and people-watch before the movie. The Broadway neighborhood has lost a bit of its luster in the past few years, but there is still a vibrancy about it.

Unlatching my seat belt, I move to get out. Instead of mimicking me, Arnie is still, staring at the four-story home that was built in the 1900s. It's far too big for the Barrington family.

"I haven't been down this street since we were all thrown out of the party," Arnie says.

I groan and collapse back against my seat, not looking at him. "Oh my god, I thought you'd forgotten! Holy crap."

Arnie turns and stares at me, eyes wide, incredulous. "I thought *you* forgot me. You never said anything."

"*You* never said anything," I respond, my tone slightly accusing.

"Is there established etiquette for that? 'Oh, hey, guy I banged years ago and never saw again, here you are!' I don't think there is." Arnie crosses his arms over his chest, slumping down in his seat. "I'm so embarrassed."

I twist around so I can see his face clearly. "Why are you embarrassed? I'm the one who should be ashamed. That party was... out of control. I'd had way too much to drink, but I do remember you. I wasn't sure at first, but then I saw the birthmark on your arm."

He lifts his arm to look at his own birthmark as if checking it's still there. "Really?"

"Yes, really. Like I said, I thought you'd forgotten *me*."

Arnie looks at me again, his hazel eyes full of some unnamed emotion. Maybe hope, maybe fear—possibly a little of both. "That night was... incredible. Amazing. How could I?" he asks. "I may have been drunk, but"—now he looks down at his lap—"I never forgot you."

"I guess we're in the same boat, then," I say. "And even better, I then ran you over on the sidewalk—what better way to get to know someone?"

"You know," Arnie says in a speculative tone, "I've always wondered if you can actually die of mortification. I don't think I appreciate being this close to finding out." He's back to staring out the window.

We're both silent for a few moments. The atmosphere in the car seems heavy to me, filled with unasked questions. Ugh. I need to fix this somehow. "Hey," I say.

He's still looking out his window.

"Arnie," I try again, "I'm pretty sure I know a way we can

exorcise the embarrassment. In any case—it can't make it worse."

Arnie turns back to me. "I'll have you know that *this* humiliation," he waves back and forth between the two of us, "amazingly, is only second in line. My first kiss was way worse, which is saying something."

I grin. "Okay, what happened?" It is Arnie, so I'm ready for a good story. Arnie scoots around in his seat, his hazel eyes wide with amusement. His mood has shifted already, in that mercurial way he has that I find so appealing.

"Okay, so, in high school I went on this date, which from the beginning was terrible and awkward—but I'd worked hard to get this guy to go out with me, and I wasn't ending it without a kiss. Anyway... we went bowling." He gives me a stern look. "I am a damn good bowler, for your information."

"I'm probably a terrible bowler; I don't know. I've never been bowling."

Arnie gasps and mock clutches his chest. "Never been bowling? Are you... what?"

"Finish telling me the kiss story." I know Arnie well enough to know he'll veer off track if I don't prompt him.

"Oh, right, the kiss. So, we decide to go bowling, and before we get there, the guy, Hank, is telling me how he's going to beat me. And FYI, I may have a slightly competitive streak, but in any case, there was no way this guy was beating me. Honestly, I tried to lose, but he was so bad I couldn't. But I still wanted my first kiss. Hank was cute, I guess." He releases a sigh. "He played saxophone and was in band..."

"What's so embarrassing about that?"

"Wait for it. So I drive him home after, and we stop in front of his house. He's mad about losing at bowling, I know that, but he's just sitting there—so I figure, you know, now's the time, we both want it. I lean over and pucker up."

I burst out laughing. Arnie glares at me, but he's also laughing.

"Oh, it gets better. We're sitting there, a sort of horrible unwinnable detente situation: I've got my lips all ready, and Hank is staring at me, horrified, like I'm an alien."

Oh, no, I think. "Oh, no," I say out loud.

"Yes. Hank was not gay. Or, at least, he hadn't figured it out yet. And that is the story of my first kiss."

"Wait, did you get your first kiss?" I ask.

"Not that night."

Now Arnie turns toward me, his gaze piercing me with the intensity of the want and longing I see in it.

Leaning across the console (later I will remember the moment with cinematic slow-motion clarity), I keep my eyes locked on Arnie's, looking for any sign that what I'm about to do is not welcome. There aren't any. Arnie's pupils dilate, and I may forget to breathe. Then our lips touch, because Arnie leans in as well, closing the distance between us.

We're tentative with each other at first, which is funny seeing as we've had sex already. Maybe it's because it happened so long ago. Maybe we're both scared our memories won't live up to the real thing. But this... this time it's different. This kiss is the beginning of a thunderstorm. The air in the car is hot and heavy; there's lightning somewhere on the horizon, and it's drawing ever closer. I need to embrace the storm. My hand is cupping the back of Arnie's head—when did that happen?

Arnie lets out a quiet moan. His fingers grip my shoulder, urging me closer; his lips open, inviting me in. Never before have I wished more for my own place. I've never wanted to bring someone home. In the past I've been perfectly happy to go to a hookup's place and then be snug in my own bed by morning.

I want to wake up with Arnie in my bed. I want Arnie in my life.

The coffee Arnie recently drank is bitter on my tongue, along with another flavor, something sweet that I want more of. Arnie's tongue sweeps into my mouth, seeking, lapping against my lips. I groan and pull away. Arnie blinks owlishly, as dazed and confused as I feel.

"If we keep this up, we'll miss the movie. Which"—I caress the back of Arnie's neck, letting my fingers slide up into the short hair at the back of his skull—"is fine, because I've seen it loads of times. And even if I hadn't, we'd need to go back to your place, because I don't take guys to my house."

It takes a minute for Arnie to respond, as if he's weighing the different possibilities. "I want to go to the movie," he finally says. "And"—he blushes; even in the dim light of my car I see it —"my place is small. Like, really small. I'd have to make sure Duff isn't home." He shuts his eyes and continues, "I cannot un-see what happened the other night."

I let my hand fall from the back of his head and chuckle. "You walked in on Duff and someone?"

Arnie slams back against his seat in obvious disgust. "Yes. His usual no-name hookup. He didn't bother putting a note on the door or even a sock on the door handle. It was awful," he finishes with a hoarse whisper.

The ten or so blocks from my house to the movie theater is one of the best walks I've ever been on. It doesn't matter that the evening is hot and muggy for Seattle. That a million other people seem to have had the same idea and are clogging the side-walks, so Arnie and I have to dodge street musicians, families, other couples, and groups of students and friends, as well as tourists gawking at the sights.

Music of all kinds blasts from random storefronts: soulful strands of a sitar stream from a Hindustani restaurant; the Last

Record Store has its doors open, and Green Day's "American Idiot" is playing. It's a cacophony, and I love it.

None of that matters, though, because about ten strides in, Arnie's hand slips into mine. Our fingers briefly tangle before sliding together as if custom fit, one hand for the other.

TWENTY-ONE

Chapter Twenty-One—Arnie

AT THE MOVIE THEATER, I make an excuse about needing to use the restroom while Tobias waits in line for popcorn.

"They make the best popcorn here. On demand, not premade and waiting in a bin," he says as he waits behind the older man who is currently ordering. "And this is my treat, since I asked you out."

Even though he paid last time, I'm not going to argue with him. I'm too distracted, wondering if—hoping—I'll have the apartment to myself that night. I rush off, following the restroom signs. In the bathroom, after first adjusting myself, I pull my phone out of my pocket and with fumbling fingers text Duff, praying he'll answer sooner rather than later.

Arnie: WILL YOU BE HOME TONIGHT. LIKE SLEEPING AT HOME ALL NIGHT?

Almost immediately, the little dots start going back and forth across the bottom of my screen. I heave a sigh of relief. I don't know if I can sit through the movie and not know if I can bring Tobias home.

Duff: ....I really want to be difficult.

Arnie: You owe me after the other day.

Duff: *eye roll*, it's not like you don't watch porn.

Arnie: Not the same thing. I don't have to SEE the actors in real life. Please.

Duff: Fine I'll go hang out with Jacob.

Arnie: Don't come home early. In fact, don't come home.

Duff: *evil looking emoji*

Arnie: *sharp knife emoji*

TOBIAS ASKS, "So, what did you think?" as we follow the other moviegoers out into the still-warm Seattle night.

I think, even if I had been able to focus on the movie, I might not have an answer. I go with, "I liked the Italian guy. He ended up being the hero. At least in my opinion."

Tobias snickers. "You hated it."

"I didn't hate it!" I protest. "I liked it, but I think I need to see it a few more times."

My attention on the movie hadn't been helped by Tobias holding my hand through the entire film, or the way our shoulders rubbed together and sent sparks down my arm, or the way Tobias kept leaning over and whispering into my ear when he wanted to explain something. And I let him. If the theater hadn't been almost full... I can't finish my thought. I'm mush. I must be, otherwise Tobias's whispering would have irritated me.

Side by side, holding hands again because the Broadway neighborhood is awesome like that, we begin to walk north. I'm trying to sort out how to casually invite Tobias to my apartment while I also try to focus on what he's telling me about *Down by Law* and the director, Jim Jarmusch. I figure I'm just going to have to watch the movie again on my own.

"He's the main reason I got interested in writing screenplays. But I also like Wim Wenders, Christopher Guest, the Coen brothers—there's a ton more who are incredible."

"That's cool." I want to know everything about Tobias. The real Tobias is so different from the imaginary one I built up in my head over the years. "What about your job now?"

"I hate working for my dad," Tobias answers. "But... I don't want to ruin the evening talking about the job or him. Want to stop here for a drink?"

I need to tell Tobias about my new job, but I don't want to ruin our evening either. *Here* is the De Luxe, a place I've never been to even though it's been in business since before I was born, the outside canopy declaring to everyone who passes by, "Since 1962."

"Sure."

"You don't sound too excited."

We stop walking. I'm trying to figure out how to ask him over without sounding totally pathetic.

I'm not cool. I'm not suave or polished, and I don't have any idea what I'm doing (both tonight and in general). But I want Tobias to come home with me. You're supposed to be getting revenge, the little voice in my head reminds me. I shove the thought aside. Revenge is the last thing on my mind right now. That ship has sailed. Being with Tobias isn't about getting revenge or cosmic justice anymore—if it ever was.

"A drink sounds nice, but..." I'm fumbling my words, but I keep going. "I... do you want to come back to my place? Duff's not home tonight. I made sure."

I know I'm blushing a bright, hot red as I force the words

out, but if I don't ask, I will never forgive myself. Never, never, never. Ever.

With a grin, Tobias tugs me out of the way of the foot traffic. "I'd love to come over. Are you sure?"

"Oh, yes. I am very, very, sure." My cheeks are still burning, but I return his grin.

There's no stopping me now; I might as well humiliate myself completely. I've had a partial erection for hours. I've told Tobias the story about Hank the band kid. There's not much lower I can go. Well, I'm sure Duff could think of an event I've forgotten about, but luckily, I've made sure he won't be home.

"Should we grab a bite to eat first? Or was popcorn and Mike and Ikes enough for now?" Tobias asks.

I grab Tobias's hand and drag him down the street and away from the De Luxe. "Next time."

Tobias laughs, trailing after me down the sidewalk.

I announce, "You know, you ruined Dick's for me for years." I am hungry, after all, and we passed the famous hamburger stand a few blocks back.

"Excuse me?"

I look over my shoulder just as Tobias nearly trips over a crack in the sidewalk. "I ruined dicks for you? Somehow I don't think so."

I stare at him, dramatically widening my eyes as far as they will go. "*Dick's*, not dicks. You're as bad as Duff. I mean the burger place, not, *you know*." I grab my package to demonstrate exactly what I mean, just as a couple of guys turn the corner heading toward us. They stare at Tobias and me. As they pass by, one of them mutters, "I'd say a four."

"Oh my god, I can't believe I did that," I say to Tobias. At their retreating backs, I yell, "What do you mean 'a four'? These skinny jeans make me look awesome!"

Tobias snickers and grabs my hand again, drawing me close

to his side. "Okay, so tell me more about your problem with Dick's."

I laugh and roll my eyes but end up telling him about how I haven't been able to eat there since the party.

"Hopefully tonight will change that." Tobias waggles his eyebrows. It's ridiculously suggestive and makes me want to grab him and kiss him right there. "We'll get you back on dicks. It's the least I can do."

I've created a monster.

I'M TRYING to turn my key in the lock, but Tobias is pressing up behind me, making it very difficult (impossible) to concentrate. Opening a door should not be this hard. Hard. I can feel Tobias's erection against my ass through both our jeans, and I shiver in anticipation. I'm getting a replay. The ref called back the ball, and I'm getting another chance. *Revenge*, the pesky voice in my head murmurs. That voice is getting quieter, and I'm having a hard time remembering what was so important about my plan. Maybe nothing.

Finally, the lock clicks over and I push the door open. The studio is dark, and best of all there is no sign of Duff. He even picked up the random clothes that are often lying around, draped over the back of the futon, or in a heap on the floor. I toss my keys onto the tiny kitchen table and flick on the overhead light.

"Nice place," Tobias says as he closes the door.

"It's small, but I like it. And between the two of us, Duff and I can afford it."

"Hey," Tobias says, his tone serious. "I need to tell you something."

I freeze, my stomach sinking through the floor and deeper, to sediment created sometime during the Proterozoic Eon.

Slowly I turn to stare at Tobias. "What?" Somehow, I'm sure he's found out about the plan. And worse, the job. Why did he wait this long to bring it up?

"Charley Hunter is just a friend. A good friend, but only a friend."

Relief floods my body, leaving me breathless. More breathless. Without air in my lungs.

Tobias doesn't know about the plan. The plan I'm going to need to tell him about at some point, but now is not the right time. Maybe I can just never admit to him what I'd been planning? The whole idea was misguided—just like Duff said.

"I figured. He's still a jerk, though."

Tobias laughs. "He can be a jerk, and he seems to know how to get under your skin."

"I don't want to talk about Charley."

"What *do* you want to talk about?" Tobias asks.

I don't think he wants me to answer. "I don't really want to talk. I'm thinking actions speak louder than words."

I want to get naked. I want to do carnal things to Tobias Barrington and have him do them back to me. But the gulf between standing in the kitchen and lying together naked on my futon seems wider and deeper than the Grand Canyon.

Why is my brain fixating on geology tonight, when I have Tobias Barrington alone in my apartment?

A wicked expression flickers across Tobias's face. I like it. He crosses from the front door to where I wait, trapping me in the kitchenette. He slowly begins unbuttoning his shirt to reveal his mostly smooth, pale chest. My gaze is drawn to the barely there chest hair that circles his nipples before coalescing above his ribs and heading south.

"Shhhoot," I manage as I snap out of my daze to hastily pull my T-shirt off over my head and throw it on the floor. I don't want to miss any part of this. I've been fantasizing about the body under Tobias's clothes for weeks, months… years.

I stare up into Tobias's eyes, my entire body feeling like it's on fire.

"It this okay?" Tobias asks.

I almost say, "What?" but Tobias's lips cover mine before I can speak, thankfully. I release a quiet sigh. Tobias feels so incredibly *right*. His mouth fits perfectly against mine, sending scorching flames of want blazing up and down my spine. I shudder against him.

Oh, god.

I part my lips so I can taste Tobias, my hands moving up to clutch his shoulders and pull him even closer. Shamelessly, I invite Tobias in to ravage me, wanting it all. I couldn't stop my body's response even if I wanted to. The sensations are too much and not enough.

Tobias's hot tongue licks into my mouth, against my teeth and the roof of my mouth. My erection throbs. God, I'm going to come from just this, standing upright in the kitchen rubbing against him.

"Bed," I manage to gasp as Tobias leaves my mouth and begins to mouth my neck like it's a banquet and he's a starving man.

I pull back, putting an inch or two of space between us. It's far too much, but I need to get naked. Stumbling from the kitchen, I manage to toe my Converse off before collapsing onto my futon, legs splayed shamelessly. Tobias stares at me for a moment, and I wonder if he likes what he sees. My gaze drifts downward from his handsome face to the bulge in his jeans. I think the answer is yes.

"I want to feel you. Taste you."

Yes, yes, yes.

I lift my hips and attempt to shimmy sexily out of my jeans

and boxers. Note to self: skinny jeans are almost impossible to get off when you have a hard-on. Smiling, Tobias leans down and tugs at the hems. I straighten my legs, and the jeans slide off along with my boxers. My cock makes a dramatic appearance, springing upward and pointing directly at Tobias like some sort of compass. A dick compass.

Tobias climbs onto the mattress, caging my legs between his and gently kissing my bobbing erection, licking off the pulse of moisture that is my body's response to his nearness. I moan. My balls are already tight. I'm not sure how long I'm going to last. It's not like I have sex every day of the week, and having this sexy man in my bed is pushing me to the edge.

It's Tobias who moans now. He opens his mouth wider and closes his lips around me, sucking on me. I watch through half-open eyes. Tobias's lips are stretched around my cock. It's obscene and a fucking turn-on. The molten heat of his mouth is propelling me closer and closer to coming. I groan and try not to thrust my cock down his throat. I've been craving more of Tobias's touch since our kiss earlier. My erection never truly fully subsided, and I don't know how long I'll be able to control myself. My hips thrust of their own volition; I *need* more of Tobias's mouth.

"Oh, god, please. I mean—Tobias." My hands land on Tobias's head, his curls soft under my fingers as I try to push him away before I come.

With porn-like grace, Tobias releases my erection, slowly letting it slide from his mouth until it snaps back against my stomach. "You don't like?"

"I do like. I like too much," I gasp. "I want you naked too. Please."

I feel a chill when Tobias crawls off the futon, but it is immediately followed by heat as he strips out of his slacks and black boxer briefs.

Tobias is as aroused as I am. He has a nice-sized cock. It lists slightly to the left—just like mine. While I appreciate nine-inch cocks when I watch porn, I don't want one up my ass.

"Come back," I plead.

Tobias covers me with his body, velvet against my starved skin. I can't help arching upward against him. Our erections bump, and it feels magical. Hooking a leg around Tobias's calf, I try for better purchase. Tobias moans and begins feasting on my neck again, nibbling before sucking, then licking to soothe the molten spots.

My hands roam at will as I writhe underneath him. I'm trying to feel everything all at once. Tobias lifts his hips and shifts to one side so he can hold our erections in his hand. Our cocks slide back and forth, driving me closer and closer to orgasm. Frotting is something I haven't done much before now. Looking between our bodies, I watch Tobias slowly jerk us together, precome making us both slick and silky. A bead of fluid pulses from Tobias's head, and the spark I've been ignoring —or just lazily riding for a few minutes—suddenly becomes impossible to ignore.

"I can't—"

Before I can finish my sentence—trying to tell Tobias I'm about to come—Tobias grunts and shoves himself hard against me. Streams of come pool on my abdomen. It's so incredibly hot. My eyes clamp shut as I follow Tobias, the electric sensation at the base of my spine and balls no longer deniable. Tobias pumps us one more time and sucks on my neck again as I come, pulsing into his hand.

I must have forgotten to breathe, because I feel lightheaded when I manage to pry my eyes open. Tobias is watching me, a bemused expression on his face.

"Was that okay?" he whispers.

"God, yes," I whisper back.

"Sorry, I was so worked up I couldn't wait."

"It was perfect," I assure him.

"I'd like to go further; I know you'd feel amazing around me."

My cock twitches in agreement. Not only would I like Tobias in me, I want to bury myself in him. "I don't have any condoms."

The smile Tobias gives me is pure gold. "Next time we'll be better prepared."

We lie there a few minutes before I untangle myself and stumble to the bathroom to grab a warm washcloth. When I return, Tobias is spread out on the futon, not even the sheet covering him. I take a moment to admire his form. He's long and lean, with broad shoulders that seem to take up most of the bed. His dark hair is tousled, and his eyes are half-shut.

"Come back here," he says, beckoning me with a twitch of a finger.

I cross the small space to kneel on the bed. Slowly and carefully I clean us up, then toss the cloth onto a pile of dirty clothes.

Lying back down, I scoot so my head rests against Tobias's chest. The steady thump of his heartbeat is reassuring. Tobias wraps his arms about me, and we lie like this for what seems like hours, slipping in and out of sleep. I've never felt happier.

Eventually the words I don't want to hear are spoken. "I have to go. Work tomorrow, and I can't be late because my dad is already pissed at me," Tobias murmurs.

Reality crashes in. I slump away from him, back onto the slightly sweaty sheets, wondering what he will think of me when I show up at Barrington Properties in a few days. I open my mouth again, to confess everything, but the words won't come. I am such a fucking coward.

TWENTY-TWO

Chapter Twenty-Two—Arnie

"WHAT ARE *YOU* DOING HERE?" Charley Hunter demands, glaring at me from across the lobby of the building Barrington Properties inhabits. One of the two elevators arrives, slides its door open, and vomits out a group of suit-clad men and women who move around us and head outside.

Of course I would run into a friend of Tobias's. Seattle is a surprisingly small city sometimes. But why does it have to be Charley? Doesn't Tobias have other, nicer friends?

As always, Charley looks like he's stepped off the page of a fashion magazine, with his linen slacks and artfully untucked cotton shirt. This in itself is funny, because Duff is an actual model, and he usually looks like he's gone to bed with wet hair and dressed in the dark—and yet, both men and women flock to him.

I shake my head. Duff is not the issue right now. I stare at Tobias's... friend. Why is Charley here?

Charley stares back at me, waiting for my answer.

"Um…" I shift and squeak before clearing my throat. "First day at my new job?"

Unlike Charley, who looks cool as a cucumber, my new suit makes me feel self-conscious and twitchy. What am I even thinking? I'll never fit into the corporate world—or even a Fortune 500–wannabe company like Barrington Properties.

Charley narrows his eyes. "Why. Are. You. Here, coffee boy?"

I stiffen my spine, refusing to let him get to me. I appreciate that he's trying to protect Tobias, but I'm not here to do him harm. "What's it to you? I'm qualified to do research. Coffee isn't my only skill."

"Oh?" Charley steps closer so we're almost chest to chest. Even though he and I are the same height, Charley manages to sneer at me down his perfectly straight nose.

"What's it to you anyway?" I repeat.

"I'm surprised to see you here. Seeing as I just left Tobias upstairs in his office getting ready to meet his new 'assistant.'" Charley raises his hands, making air quotes with his fingers. "The one his father hired for him. That wouldn't be you, would it? You would've told Tobias you were applying to Barrington, right? On your date the other night."

I open and close my mouth. I want to defend myself. The other night was so much more than a date, and for some reason it's important to me that Charley Hunter know this. Tobias has been busy the past week, but we've texted a few times. Tobias told me some funny stories about other people at these networking events he's being forced to attend and sent me dick puns, making me regret telling him my Dick's story. Not really, though. Tobias even asked how my job search was going. And each time I started to reply to tell him I'd been hired at Barring-ton, I froze and deleted the words.

"I… it never came up," is my reply. It's a lie of omission, but a lie nonetheless. I don't know how to tell Tobias, and this morning I'd hoped I wouldn't run into him and somehow things would explain themselves.

Because that always works out.

Charley steps closer to me, his nostrils flaring and his cheeks ever-so-slightly flushed. "Tobias is my best friend. Do not fuck with him. Andrew Barrington is a jackass who wants to control him. If he's hired you to keep an eye on Tobes—"

My eyes widen. "No! I'm supposed to be helping with research or something, mortgage histories and stuff like that, very basic. No one's told me anything about Tobias. I don't know who I'm working with. Jesus. Do you think my job is really to spy on Tobias?"

Charley shrugs, stepping back and giving me a little more room to breathe. "Tobias's father is a piece of work. I wouldn't put it past him to hire someone he thinks he can use to get to his son—even more than he already does. But..." Charley looks me up and down, seeming to come to some sort of decision. "Maybe you're perfect. Tobias likes you. Don't fuck it up." The last part is only a tiny bit menacing. What does Charley think he can do?

"I should get going. I'm late, no thanks to you." I start to move toward the elevators. I wonder what Charley meant when he said I was perfect. Perfect how? A perfect fuckup?

Charley lifts his hand, palm out, stopping me from stepping onto the elevator that has just arrived again. I look around, wondering where the stairs are. With my luck this morning, the elevator is going to get stuck anyway.

"Just a sec. I want to try something. Call reception and tell them you're going to be late—that there's an accident on I-5."

"But why? I'm right here. I took the bus! I don't even own a car."

"They don't know that. Just do it."

Sure, I think, dragging my phone out of my suit pocket. I'll be like Nike and *just do it*. Which begs the question, why am I listening to Charley when I'm already late? The phone rings at the other end. When the receptionist answers, I make a stumbling apology about the fictitious accident on I-5, telling her I'll be there as soon as possible.

"Happy now?" I shove my phone back into my pocket.

"Just wait. I want to know if I'm right."

"No one ever said anything about who I would be working for," I mutter, irritated and confused. "When I interviewed, it sounded like I'd be assisting more than one person."

Pulling his own phone out, Charley taps the screen and holds it up to his ear.

"Hey, Tobes, sorry to bug you again. I know you're busy... Oh, the new guy is late? Huh, that's too bad—probably a flake." He raises an irritatingly perfect eyebrow in my direction. "Did you get tickets to the fall film festival yet? You did? Nice. Later." Charley slips his phone back into his pocket and cocks his head at me. "Ball's in your court." Without a backward glance, he walks off, pushing his way through the lobby doors out onto Eastlake and disappearing into the early-lunch crowd.

"Asshole," I grumble.

I feel like a mixed-up Cinderella—all dressed up with nowhere to go. I have both shoes, lucky me, but the ball is ending at midnight, and I need to... do *something*, or everything is going to fall apart. Should I go upstairs or not?

I'm paralyzed by indecision long enough that the elevators come and go several times. Strangers move past me as they go about their daily business; I'm still unable to decide what the right thing to do is.

Dammit, if Charley is by chance right, I don't want some stranger hired by Tobias's dad to spy on him. If anyone is going to be spying, it will be me. And I need to tell Tobias the truth, today. Everything.

I stare at the elevator doors, my resolve firming. I'm going to ride the damn thing upstairs, and, if they don't fire me on the spot for being late, I'll see what I can do to fix this situation. Who knows, maybe I'm making a mountain out of a molehill. Maybe Tobias won't think it's weird that I applied and got a job at Barrington Properties—without telling him every single time I had a chance to.

Anyway, why can't Tobias and I work together? Maybe he and I can—I jab the Up button impatiently—turn the tables on Andrew Barrington if it turns out he is up to no good. Personally, after my research on the elder Barrington, I think he should worry more about his own life than his son's—but what do I know?

I know it's time to come clean with Tobias. I'm done lying. I think the only person who fell for this scheme of mine was me.

TWENTY-THREE

Chapter Twenty-Three—Tobias

"THE NEW HIRE IS HERE." Carly's voice crackles over my intercom, a relic from the early 2000s. "I'm giving him a tour, taking him to meet Mr. Barrington, and then bringing him to you."

Great. I'm already in a crap mood because I've been forced to go to networking events the past two evenings and they ended too late for me to show up afterward at Arnie's apartment. And Arnie's been working a lot, or busy, anyway, and sounds stressed out when we manage to talk on the phone.

All I want to do is hang out with Arnie and to get to know him better. I want to learn the things boyfriends are supposed to know, like his favorite food, his favorite color. Is he a morning person; does he like pineapple on pizza?

I know it's ridiculous, but... are Arnie and I officially boyfriends? That's what I want, and I think Arnie does too. I'm terrible at being a casual boyfriend. Jonas, my only serious boyfriend, told me I was "too possessive" before dumping me. I guess if possessive means I want to spend time with my boyfriend, share dreams, do day-to-day stuff together, then I am possessive.

My email chimes, reminding me I'm supposed to be working. My father has sent over a file, via Carly because he can't bring himself to send the paperwork directly to me or walk it down the hall, for crying out loud, for a sale that's closing in the next few days. Sighing, I click on it and begin reading it over, making sure all the i's have been dotted and t's crossed. It's tedious, but it needs to be done. As my dad always says, mistakes are expensive.

A tap on my door startles me. "Come in."

Carly pushes it open, motioning to someone behind her. "Come on in and meet Tobias." Carly is a few years older than me. She's a single mom who works her ass off for Barrington and is also taking evening classes to become a paralegal. I think she should go to law school, but she seems to think she isn't smart enough.

"Oh, um, hey," says a voice I recognize. "Tobias and I know each other."

Arnie slips past Carly and into my office space. He sounds like the Arnie I know, but he looks... well, he's wearing a suit instead of a T-shirt and jeans, and he's gotten a haircut too. His hair is styled into something that doesn't look permanently windblown.

I stand up too quickly, and the floor seems to move underneath my feet. I clutch at the desk to regain my balance.

Carly glances between us. I don't know what she sees, or thinks she sees, but Carly doesn't miss much.

"I'll just leave you two to... get more acquainted," she says as she leaves, pulling the door shut behind her.

"What are you... Why are you here?" I ask.

These worlds of mine colliding feels... off. I have my work

world, which I despise, and the Arnie world, which makes everything better. And, yes, the Arnie world is new to me, but I crave it already. Arnie is everything Charley had said he was, a bit weird and socially awkward, but he fits *my* weird and awkward like a glove—or wears the matching one to mine.

"This is awkward," he says quietly.

"For you or for me? More awkward than the kiss story you told the other night?"

"Absolutely, undeniably," he assures me.

I stare at my... assistant? Boyfriend? I have to admit Arnie looks great in the suit he's wearing. It's not Armani, but he's had it altered to fit his slender form, and it looks amazing. The subtle gray-blue makes his hazel eyes and the auburn highlights in his hair pop.

"Do you mind if we sit down? Or"—he glances out the window behind me—"we could maybe go for a walk, like all the other suits do at lunchtime."

A walk. How many times in the past few days have I wished he could meet me for lunch and we could spend some time together? At least one hundred.

"A walk would be nice," I respond.

Arnie bows. "Lead the way."

WE DON'T TALK as the elevator transports us to the ground floor. I don't know what to say. I have no idea why Arnie is so quiet. And still no clue what he's doing here at Barrington Properties.

It's two short blocks to the walking path alongside Lake Union. The sun is bright, warming my shoulders. I reach up and loosen my collar. Arnie walks next to me, our arms bumping occasionally. I sense he's nervous about something.

The fluttery feeling in my stomach refuses to go away. In

fact, the longer we walk without speaking, the worse it gets. I'm a writer. I can imagine a lot of scenarios. Are we... breaking up? We're not really together yet, so I abandon that idea. Did he use my name to get the job? I actually can't imagine this happening. My father or Carly would've said something. Besides, Arnie could work anywhere he wants. He has a degree in data science or something like that. And Latin, which I think is very cool. The only foreign language I speak is pig latin.

"So," Arnie begins, sending me a sideways glance, "you're probably wondering what's going on. Why I showed up at your office."

I nod vehemently. "That's an understatement, really."

Arnie blows out a deep breath. "We kind of have to go back a ways for me to explain. And apologize."

We reach the footpath that runs along the east side of the lake. It's wide enough for us to walk side by side, although it's busy today with the other lunchtime walkers Arnie mentioned. The weather is still warm, but I think I can feel that slight change, a dip in temperature that means fall—my favorite season—is on its way. Maybe Arnie and I—no, I can't think about fall. I need to focus on what's happening now.

"Okay, start talking," I say.

Lake Union sparkles under the late-summer sunshine. It's still a working lake, with loads of piers and boathouses pinned to its shores. Among these marine businesses are interspersed groups of floating homes, some of which date back to the early 1920s. I dream of living in one someday. Even in chilly winter, it seems like a sort of freedom to be that close to the water all the time.

"So, back to the party, in high school. Duff and I were there, as you know."

Ah, the party. I didn't know Duff had been there too. I'd only had eyes for Arnie.

I frown and open my mouth to say something, I'm not sure what, but Arnie stops me with a raised hand.

"Going to the party was the most daring thing I'd ever done, and when you looked at me... Not just once or twice; you *looked* at me, and then... you know." His hand flutters, and I allow a small grin to form, because I do know.

"But then the party broke up, and I never saw you again. I figured you didn't care about a guy like me, a guy who'd never had sex before. Until then I'd only kissed like four people. Fast forward to today and me still being a loser. I'm not saying I pined over you or anything, but... well." He sighs. "I guess I *did* pine. That's me, Arnie the piner. The minute I saw your name in bold on your credit card that day, I should've realized I'd been pining—but I'm clueless.

"Anyway, looking back over the past few years I— Boy, you know? Duff told me it was a lousy idea. Um, where was I? Oh, right, so when you started coming into the Buzz, everything came back to me. Add in making me wear my coffee that one morning, and I was just so mad. After all this time, here I am working at a café, and you're successful... it seemed like the thing to do was even the scales a bit, so I decided to get revenge. And then of course there was the unrecognized pining.

"I was going to even the scales, teach you a lesson. But in order to do that, I had to get a better job and stuff, so you'd like me. I applied around, and, honestly, yes, I applied here"—he waves backward, in the general direction of Barrington—"because of you. But I had no idea I might be working for you, and now everything is completely awkward. And I want you to know, along the way you became real to me, not the Tobias Barrington I'd built up in my head. I'm sorry for weirdly going behind your back. I know I should have told you before now. I just couldn't figure out what to say. Have you ever read *Harriet the Spy*?"

"Um, no?"

"It's a kids' book from the '60s. My mom and I read it together. Anyway, I feel a bit like Harriet did when she lost her notebook. Which... makes no sense to you, because you haven't read the book." He shakes his head. "It doesn't matter. I just want you to know, I've really liked getting to know you, and I understand if you want to—not see each other anymore."

I nod, but something else Arnie said niggles at me. "I was your first?" I ask.

I'd been inexperienced back then too. Poor Arnie. I still cringe when I remember the drunken fumbling that had ended up with us in bed together, limbs tangled, come all over both our bodies. Good god. Although obviously it had not been forgotten, so maybe it had been good.

He whispers, quietly enough I almost don't hear him over the thrum of traffic, "I'm ashamed. And I'm sorry too, for everything. It's probably medically dangerous to be this embarrassed." He looks at me, the corners of his eyes crinkling. "I just keep pushing the envelope of shame. Who knew it was possible?"

Arnie stops walking, moving to one side of the path where there's a little space to stand out of the way of people. I follow, of course, and stop by his side.

Looking into my eyes, Arnie utters the very words I know I'm not ready to hear. "I'll quit. I'll leave now, and you can tell Carly that it didn't work out, that you couldn't work with me. What I did was wrong."

I should be angry about what Arnie's done, right? But hadn't I tried to use Charley to make Arnie jealous? Hadn't I had a plot of my own, a counterplot, when I could've just straightforwardly asked him out? And I had been paying attention to my phone and not my feet, resulting in a coffee disaster that had taken me weeks to apologize for. Maybe I hadn't been planning revenge—I huff out a strangled laugh—but I hadn't exactly been direct.

"What? What's funny?" Arnie demands.

He's adorable, half righteous and half apologetic. He's been running his hand through his hair, and whatever product he'd used to keep it in order has given up completely.

"You're funny. I'm funny. This whole thing is funny. I should probably tell you now that I purposely brought Charley into the coffee shop to make you jealous."

"It worked," Arnie mutters darkly. Then he adds, "I saw him in the lobby today," the word *him* uttered the same way someone might say "the bubonic plague." "He asked if I was hired to spy on you or control you somehow. Is that something your dad would do? Because, unlike Harriet, I am obviously the world's worst spy."

Did my father hire Arnie to keep an eye on me? It's possible, I suppose, but I don't think so. I do believe Arnie's been hired to help with my workload. The fact that he's my boyfriend is a perk my dad doesn't know, yet.

"I don't think so," I reply. "My dad is just... He'd like to control everything I do." I shrug, adding, "But I only have seven more months until I can tell him to screw off, so I'm not worried."

"Why is that?"

"Come on." I gesture toward the lake and step back onto the path. Arnie follows me while I decide how much to tell him. The thing is, I trust Arnie. I've learned the hard way that there are a lot of guys out there who will do anything, even pretend to like me, just because I have money. Money I don't have access to yet. Maybe my grandmother had the right idea making me wait until I turn twenty-five and have a better idea of what I want to do with my life.

"So," I say, "in seven months from now, I'll get an inheritance from my grandmother. It's held in trust until I turn twenty-five."

"Wow, inheritance. That's cool. My mom always says I'll be lucky if I get a penny, because she's going to spend it all. And my dad wouldn't leave me a dirty rag."

Arnie stops walking again, forcing the other walkers to move around us. "Can I ask you something?" He's peering up at me, a serious expression on his face.

"Sure."

"Are we, like, okay? Because, even though this"—he swirls his hand between us—"started out as a harebrained plan, I really, really like you, and I'm really, really sorry." His cheeks flush bright red again he shifts from side to side, looking like if he wants to run far away. He won't get far in his shiny new shoes.

I cock my head to one side, looking down into Arnie's eyes as if maybe the right answer will appear there. Are we okay? I think so. I like Arnie a lot, and his "plot" brought us together, so what's the problem? The past few days all I've done is think about him and the movie night that ended up with the two of us in bed together.

"Are there any other secret plans you aren't telling me?" I squint menacingly, trying to think of something outrageous he might have planned. Something Arnie-like. "Maybe this is part of the plot. You're getting close to me so you can access the safe code and rob Barrington Properties of every penny." There's no safe, but Arnie doesn't know that. Besides, I enjoy the mental image of Arnie dressed up like a cat burglar.

Arnie's face actually turns ashen, and he grabs my sleeve—in panic, I think. "What? No! But I did ask Gale to get Charley to go to the block party with Duff, except I called it off. I only wanted to get my V-card back, see. Okay, yeah, ridiculous, right? I know that's not possible. But I thought if I got something from you that was equal in value to my V-card. Like, your heart, which now that I think about it is totally ridiculous, because your heart is way more valuable than my V-card. And you have no idea about any of this. How could you? You didn't know me, and I didn't know you. There was nothing to know. There is no knowing. So, your heart, way more valuable than my V-card, not equal at all, and—"

I can't hold it back. The first chuckle escapes, and before I know it, I'm laughing and laughing until my stomach muscles start to complain. Tears of laughter stream down my face, and I actually have to bend over and rest my forearms on my knees while strangers walking along the path shoot me funny looks. Finally I'm able to get myself under control. I stand back up and check out Arnie. He's watching me with a resigned air.

"Are you finished now?" he asks.

I wipe my eyes. "Oh my god." I have to take another deep breath to stop the last chuckle threatening to escape. "Yeah, I think so," I reply.

Chapter Twenty-Four—Arnie

I CONTEMPLATE WALKING HOME. If I weren't wearing the world's most uncomfortable shoes, I would.

It's weird how hindsight is so clear. Why did I go through with the job after getting to know Tobias? Why didn't I leave well enough alone and just wait until I had an interview at another company? I still can, I reason. If Barrington wanted to hire me, surely there are other companies—companies Tobias Barrington does not work at—that need someone like me. One thing I've figured out while I've been shenanigans-ing about is, I do want to get a better job and move on with my life. A years-ago encounter with Tobias has nothing to do with where I am now. Not really.

But noooo, I went through with the plan and damned the consequences. I let myself get carried away with the idea of cosmic fairness.

Well, there is cosmic fairness, isn't there, and it's called...

Consequences.

Is the word hanging above my head writ in neon letters? No? It sure feels like it to me.

As I wait for my bus, I scuff my toe at a piece of gravel, kicking it and watching as the rock skitters out into the street. A car drives past, its front tire rolling over the gravel and causing it to pop back toward the sidewalk. I know just how the rock feels. Or I would if rocks had feelings.

I realize with a sickening thud of my heart—I've gone and fallen in... *like* with Tobias Barrington. What I feel is *like*, and that's all, dammit. *Like* is something I can recover from; I'm not thinking about the other word.

So what if we've gone to the movies and held hands as we walked along Broadway? So what if my mom texted me to tell Tobias how much she'd liked him? None of it matters.

I spot the bus in the distance, barreling down Eastlake, a cloud of dust and diesel fumes following behind it. It's packed with rush hour commuters, and I have to stand the entire ride, my uncomfortable shoes pinching my toes.

Instead of taking it all the way to my studio, though, I get off at the stop nearest to the Buzz. With any luck, Gale will be there and I can ask for my old job back. Regardless of what Tobias said, things between us are not okay, I just know it. If things were okay, he'd would've said goodbye before he left.

"WHAT DO you mean you hired someone to take my position already?" I hate how my voice squeaks.

Gale looks apologetic but shrugs. "Did you think I was going to wait and see if your new job worked out for you, Arnie? If you want, I can probably give you a Sunday shift, but that's it."

I don't want a Sunday shift. I want never to have been so outrageous in the first place. I want never to have lied and tricked Tobias. Tears threaten. I blink and take a deep breath, forcing them back.

"Is the work that bad? Are you sure you aren't being, maybe, dramatic about Tobias? I imagine it was a surprise for him to see you there," Gale says.

There's no way I'm being dramatic; why would she think that?

I ponder Gale's question for a second. In actuality, the work is something I'd enjoy. I spent the afternoon with Carly learning how to research properties: how to use the county database to discover liens, if there was more than one owner, mortgage balances, that sort of thing. It's a bit like being a detective. Much of what I'm supposed to do is look over submitted appraisals and see if they're realistic: Will a bank accept it to support a loan? Did the appraiser leave something out or add too much to increase the value of a property? Is the property map correct? If not, then we would ask the appraiser to reevaluate. I'd liked it, enjoyed it even. Except for the fact that Tobias's office door remained stubbornly closed every time I passed by, and when it came time to leave for the day, I never saw him. I must have looked pathetic, because, finally, Carly told me he'd left in a hurry.

I resist checking my phone again.

"The work is fine," I say.

"So, do you want a Sunday shift?" Gale asks.

"No, but thanks."

"Do you want to tell me what happened?"

I sigh. I've been doing that a lot and can't seem to stop myself, although I haven't managed to hyperventilate yet. "Tobias found out about everything. I mean, he found out because I told him. But it was awkward and kind of horrible."

Gale nods, her expression one of sympathy now. "Was he

mean about it? That doesn't seem like him to me. I don't know him that well, but he's never struck me as cruel or vindictive."

"No, he was actually pretty understanding. But..."

"But?"

"But," I waggle my head, really wishing I'd gone straight home instead of stopping by to further embarrass myself in front of Gale, "he can't trust me now."

"I'm sorry, sweetie. I think you're wrong, though."

Ugh, having Gale be nice and understanding is almost as bad as having Tobias be nice and understanding. I wonder if I can feel any lower.

The answer is yes, of course. I just don't know it yet. It's not until later in the evening, after I've taken a shower and changed into my most comfortable moping clothes, that the final blow comes.

I'm indulging myself by binge-watching *The Big Bang Theory* on my laptop, enjoying someone else's social mishaps, when my cell phone rings. There is no way it's Tobias, even though I hope it will be. Duff rarely calls or texts; he just shows up when he feels like it. This means the call is from my mother or a telemarketer. Setting my laptop aside, I dig my phone out from underneath my pillow and check the screen.

"Hi, hon!"

"Hi, Mom."

"You didn't call today; I want to hear all about it. And I have some news for you too!"

I almost ask, "Hear all about what?" before I realize she wants to know about my first day at work.

"It was fine," I lie. Today has been the most humiliating day of my life, and that's surprising when I think back on some of the things I've done.

"What happened?"

In the past, I appreciated my mother's ability to know when

something is wrong, so I didn't have to explain myself—but not any longer.

"Nothing happened. It was fine. I met a lot of people, had a tour in the morning, and then in the afternoon I started doing some training. They're going to have me take some classes too."

"Are they paying for them? Don't you let that Andrew Barrington push you around."

"Yes, they're paying for them. Jeez, he's not pushing me around."

But I wonder about that, since Charley had said something like that too.

"I just can't imagine he's changed much. People don't, you know."

"Whatever happened between you and Andrew Barrington, anyway?" I ask.

She hedges. "It was a long time ago."

"Yes, Mom, I know, when dinosaurs roamed the earth."

That makes her chuckle. "They were so colorful. Some had feathers!"

"And you walked to school uphill both directions, in the snow."

"I did! Your grandmother, bless her heart, would pack me a little sack lunch every day, and by the time I'd gotten to school I would've eaten it, so I was starved as well."

"Mom, focus. Andrew Barrington?" I growl, distracted from my pity party.

"Oh, him. There were a few things that put him on my poop list. One, he dated a good friend of mine and cheated on her. He denied it until he was caught—red-handed, so to speak—the man put the 'gas' in 'gaslighting.' And he was accused of misappropriation of funds when he was treasurer of some campus club." She pauses. "I can't recall if the charge was ever proven, but I do remember he was asked to step down. All very hush-hush, you know, frat boys protecting frat boys."

"How did he make his money? Like to start a business and stuff." I've wondered about that, what with the big house on Capitol Hill.

"I think most of it came from that trophy wife of his. Her father owned a car dealership, several of them, and there was some real estate tossed in there too. If I recall, there's even a building in the U District called the Selznick, which must've been built by Olivia Barrington's great-grandfather or someone like that."

That explains Barrington Properties. Real estate is probably classier than car dealerships, I don't know. But, after meeting him briefly that morning, I would bet my last ten dollars that Andrew Barrington wants to be thought of as upper class.

"You seem to know an awful lot about someone you barely know."

"You forget, Seattle was a much smaller city back in my college days. Any two people born here likely ended up knowing a lot of the same people."

That is true; we'd talked about that very thing when we had dinner together. Apparently, it's a miracle Mom and Will-the-dentist hadn't met earlier in life, as they were both Seattle natives. Will, however, had grown up in south Seattle, while Mom reigned in the north.

"What was the other news you had?"

Silence.

My stomach, which is still a little queasy from my day, does an anxious flip.

"Mom," I ask, "is something wrong?"

Is she sick and hasn't told me? Cancer, or something worse?

"Will and I are getting married. He asked me this past weekend, and I accepted." She says the words really fast, as if she's afraid she won't get them out.

Definitely something worse. I mean, I'm relieved she isn't sick. In the ten seconds it took for her to answer, I'd already shot through every possible scenario of her non-illness. Marriage, though? I can't imagine it.

"You're marrying Will-the-dentist?" I blurt. I knew it. I knew she wasn't telling me something.

"Honey," Mom says in that very reasonable tone that informs me I am the one being unreasonable.

"What?"

I can't help it if the word comes out petulantly. I feel petulant. I want to be petulant. I decide that very second: I'm changing my middle name to Petulant. So there. *Petulant*. And it's dumb, because I like Will and I want my mom to be happy, to have someone like I hope to have Tobias.

"Sweetie, I am marrying Will. We want to have a get-together with everyone before the weather turns, so you can meet his daughters. He's invited you and Tobias—that's why I called; we need to figure out a good weekend for all of us."

A good weekend, hah.

There's never going to be a good weekend for Tobias and me to have dinner with them, because Tobias and I do not exist, except in my imagination. Even if Tobias says things are okay… things don't feel okay. That voice in my head reminds me what Gale said earlier: maybe you're being dramatic.

I take a deep breath and remind myself I'm happy for my mom and Will. They've found each other, and they make each other happy.

"Mom, I'm happy for you. I really am. It's just, you know, a lot."

Mom chuckles. "Arnie, you've never been a fan of change. And I know this is a big one."

"I have no idea what you're referring to." But I'm smiling as I utter the words. We both know she's right. Change is something I've always approached with great caution—which is funny, because I've just changed almost everything in my life and, remarkably, I'm still here. In fact, I might possibly have improved myself.

As long as I haven't scared Tobias away with my self-created drama.

Me, dramatic? Never.

Chapter Twenty-Five—Tobias

WHEN I GET BACK to the office after my lunch walk with Arnie, my cell phone immediately buzzes.

CHARLEY: WHAT'S THE MOST OUTRAGEOUS THING YOU'VE EVER DONE?

TOBIAS: WHAT ARE YOU TALKING ABOUT?

CHARLEY: I NEED A FAVOR.

Didn't I see Charley this morning? Why couldn't he have asked me then? Then I remember he has a "gig" in Vegas.

TOBIAS: WHAT?

I have a feeling in the pit of my stomach that tells me I'm going to regret responding.

CHARLEY: I'M IN VEGAS, I NEED HELP.

TOBIAS: ...WHY?

CHARLEY: THREE DAY CONVENTION.

CHARLEY: PLEASE. YOU OWE ME.

Charley is referring to his pretending for thirty seconds to be my boyfriend, which had fooled absolutely no one.

What could go wrong? I like Vegas enough.

CHARLEY: FLY DOWN ASAP YOU'LL BE BACK SUNDAY. I PROMISE.

TOBIAS: RIGHT NOW? TODAY?

CHARLEY: YOU OWE ME.

I do owe him; he never asks for my help. I'd planned on seeing what Arnie was doing tonight, but we were late getting back from our walk as it was, and Carly snatched him away the minute we walked through the door.

TOBIAS: DAD ISN'T GOING TO BE HAPPY.

I want to tell him about Arnie too, but it seems like maybe the wrong time. And a lot to text.

CHARLEY: SCREW YOUR DAD, WHEN HAS HE EVER DONE ANYTHING FOR YOU?

...ASIDE FROM DONATING SPERM?

TOBIAS: WHAT KIND OF CONVENTION IS IT?

CHARLEY:.......

TOBIAS:???

CHARLEY: ...ADVANCED GEOSCIENCES AND ENVIRON-MENTAL GEOLOGY.

This means only one thing: Charley's ex, Simon, is there too. Charley really does need me.

I FEEL HORRIBLY guilty running off to Vegas without saying goodbye to Arnie, without at least letting him know what's going on. I look around the office after texting with Charley, but I don't immediately spot him. He could be anywhere in the building, and I don't have any more time. My flight leaves in three hours. I barely have time to go home and grab a bag.

I tell Carly I have to leave early and race home (without hitting anything, thank you very much), gleeful I'm not attending any meetings that evening or, hopefully, ever again.

My dad is going to be pissed off and, frankly, I can't bring myself to care.

This is just the beginning of my defiance; Arnie Ferguson has loosened something in me—something that was holding me back. I can't explain it, but I know he's the cause. He's the reason I'm not afraid to drop everything.

There's a honk from outside. I look out my window and see the Lyft I called waiting for me at the curb. Quickly I toss a few more articles of clothing into my bag and zip it closed. With my carry-on in one hand, I sprint down the stairs and out the front door.

Las Vegas, here I come.

The execution of my escape is perfect, a ten out of ten, right up until I'm approaching security and try to pull up my boarding pass on my phone... which is not in my pocket. I remember with clarity, it's sitting on my bed at home, right where I tossed it in my frantic dash to pack my clothes.

Great.

I can't call or text Arnie.

Also, my dad can't call or text me. Which is a plus and almost worth forgetting my phone.

If there's some cosmic justice behind this, I don't know what it is. All I know is, now I feel like a complete jackass. I race back to one of the kiosks to print out a paper pass and manage to make it to my gate. It's going to be the longest two-and-a-half-hour flight I've ever taken.

Chapter Twenty-Six—Arnie

I SERIOUSLY CONSIDER NOT SHOWING up for work the next day. But... I need the paycheck, because I concocted the most ridiculous plan in the entire history of mankind to get Tobias's attention and, in doing so, quit the job that paid my rent. And bought groceries. And blah blah blah.

So, sadly, quitting isn't an option.

MY SECOND DAY at Barrington is much like the first, except I don't see Tobias around at all. I want to ask Carly where he is, but I also don't want to know the answer. Plus, she's busy trying to get my email and stuff set up. If Tobias is in his office and ignoring me, it would hurt even if I deserve it. I'd hoped that even if we weren't dating, we could at least be friends.

Lucky me, I've been assigned my very own cubicle among the other peons. It's one floor down from reception and faces a wall, which is unfortunate, but I don't have a neighbor (yet), which is nice. I spend the morning doing more onboarding stuff and going through the very basic training they offer online.

I'm still stewing about the Tobias situation, so just after lunch when Carly's voice comes from behind me, it startles the crap out of me. I turn around to look at her while trying to compose myself. I want so badly to ask her about Tobias, but I don't even know if she knows Tobias is gay, much less that we are—were—possibly maybe, dating. Possibly. Although the likelihood of dating seems to be going down the longer Tobias's silence lasts.

She's watching me, a thick manila file folder in her grip. By the look on her face, I'm pretty sure I haven't managed the not-panicked expression. Maybe I should quit trying to smile so much. I probably look like a constipated clown. Carly seems nice enough, and she seems familiar, but I can't place her; I figure it's one of those things where she looks like someone I've met. There's a hesitancy about her, especially after Tobias and I went on our little walk. Maybe she does keep an eye on Tobias for Andrew Barrington? I don't know, either, if Tobias is out to his family. There is so much I don't know about him, and it's driving me up a wall.

"Do you feel confident looking up these properties? The top file needs to be done today, and everyone else is busy," Carly says.

I take the stack of papers she's holding out.

"Sure?"

"These are county records searches, same as you were doing yesterday. The bottom ones aren't sales; you're verifying our records versus what the county has in their records."

That's easy enough.

I screw up my courage to ask the question that has been bugging me all day. "Is Tobias around?"

Carly shakes her head. Her red curls bounce, defying whatever hold crème she's applied. "He's off-site, I think. If you can send me the information on that one file by the time you leave today, I'd appreciate it."

I hardly hear her last words, I'm so relieved Tobias doesn't have his door shut so he can avoid contact with me. He's not avoiding me; he's not here. Carly's still watching me. If I knew her better, I'd think she wants to say something else, something not about leases, parcels, and profit percentages.

"Sure," I repeat, turning back to my monitor and setting the files next to me.

"It's boring, and the rest of them will probably take a few days. Hopefully we'll get your Barrington account set up soon so you can log in under your own profile and not as a guest, and get you a desk phone," she says as she leaves.

The research isn't terrible. It's easy. In fact, often I find myself curious and wanting to know more about the properties. I end up looking back further in time than Carly requested. It's interesting reading the names of property's previous owners, seeing when a building or home last sold and why. Sometimes it's obvious to me an owner died or a divorce forced the sale. Often, too, the county has photographs attached to the files, and I can see how the property has changed over the years.

As requested, I note where Barrington records differ, which isn't often. Barrington manages as well as buys and sells property. Some of the things I'm confirming are leases and renewal dates. Leases for homes are straightforward, but business leases have all sorts of additional bits of information. I never knew a landlord charged physical rent but also often received a percentage of the business's profit. How is that fair?

As Carly said, there are a lot of properties for me to look at. By midafternoon, I've only managed to get through about a third of the parcel numbers, although at least the work has kept me from worrying about Tobias. I've checked my phone about a zillion times, and there are no new messages.

A LITTLE AFTER FOUR, my phone vibrates. I can't get to it fast enough, but once I have it in my sweaty grip, I see it's my mom, not Tobias.

"Hi, hon."

"Heya, Mom," I say quietly, checking around myself to make sure I'm not bothering anyone around me by taking a personal call, but no one seems to notice.

"I'm just checking in. You didn't sound great last night, and I know my news was a little bombshellish."

"I'm okay. Surprised, is all." I know my mom deserves this. She's happy, and it's obvious Will thinks the world of her. It's just that we've been a team for so long, I selfishly don't want to share her with anyone. "Honestly, I'm happy for you. Really happy."

"We want to have you to dinner again so you can meet Will's girls. We'll have it at Will's house in Edmonds, something low-key and casual."

"Okay." Even though it sounds about as fun as waxing my privates. "Have you guys… set a date or anything?" I ask.

This opens the gates for every detail possible about the upcoming nuptials, which are happening in December—which seems very soon to me.

"We were thinking of having it on a boat, but we've decided on a place in Georgetown. It's perfect, Arnie, big enough for all the guests but small enough to feel intimate. There's a parquet dance floor; we're going to have a swing band."

Immediately I think about dancing with Tobias. I'm a crap dancer, but for him I would learn. I wonder if he knows stuff like the fox-trot or the Charleston? If he doesn't, will he want to take lessons together? I can almost hear the trumpet playing a solo while I hold Tobias's hand and he—

"Honey?" Mom must have said my name more than once. "Are you still there?"

"Oh, sorry. When is this dinner?"

I agree to another Saturday dinner. I must be a complete glutton for punishment. After we click off, I get back to my research. I'm deeply involved in organizing information on a property complicated by death and divorce. The small home is located in the south end in what I learn is an area once known as Garlic Gulch.

Of course, I have to find out why it was called that. I end up on Facebook reading about the history of Italians and Greeks in Seattle. There's a whole group dedicated to this part of Seattle's history: wedding photos, snapshots of businesses in the '30s and '40s. I'm completely immersed.

A tap on my shoulder about sends me to the ceiling. I've been so swept away by this fascinating bit of Seattle history I'm not aware of my surroundings, which happens when I am focused on something interesting.

I jerk and look behind me. I'm sure I look guilty as heck. But hey, not porn! Just Facebook.

It's Carly. She has a kind of funny expression on her face, one I can't read, and she's holding out a cell phone. "It's for you," she says.

I gingerly take the phone, holding the thing as if it's a live snake or, even worse, a spider. Once, when I was like eight, a friend's mom made one of those sensory boxes for a "fun" activity at a party, and we all had to put our hands inside it. I had a total meltdown and had to leave the party early. I'm not sure I've ever recovered.

"Who is it?" I ask.

Carly raises her eyebrows at me. "Why don't you answer and find out?"

I suppose that would work.

With my eyes on Carly, I slowly raise the phone to my ear. "Hello? This is Arnie Ferguson."

"Arnie! It's Tobias."

Oh my god, I am so relieved to hear his voice. I don't know what to say.

"Arnie?"

Literally don't know what to say.

"Um, hi?"

Carly shakes her head. "Bring my phone upstairs when you're finished with it," she says quietly as she walks away. I nod even though she can't see me and swing back around in my chair.

"So, funny story," Tobias says into my ear. "I'm in Vegas. And I forgot my phone at home."

"Vegas?" All I can think is, the temperature must be like nine million degrees.

"Yeah, Charley needed my help. Needs my help. He's a mess."

That I can't believe. Charley Hunter is always 100 percent on target.

"By the time I got here," Tobias continues, "he was almost too drunk to walk. But I'll tell you about that later. In my rush I forgot my phone and couldn't figure out how to get a hold of you. I used Charley's phone to call the office and get Carly's number so I could call you on it and, well, now I'm talking to you."

"I'm still trying to process the 'Charley's a mess' part."

"I'm sorry I forgot my phone. I... didn't want you to think I changed my mind or anything."

"Oh, I didn't think that," I lie.

"Pfft. You totally did." I can almost hear Tobias's smile. "We may not know everything about each other yet, but I know you that well."

"Okay, maaaybe I was a little freaked out. A tad." Even though he can't see me, I pinch my thumb and index finger together and then separate them so I create an L shape—that's how freaked out I'd been.

"So," he continues, "I'm giving Charley a hand, but I'll be home on Sunday, maybe Saturday evening. If I'm lucky?"

As I'm sitting there feeling the immense relief of knowing that Tobias hasn't changed his mind and decided I'm some sort of scary stalker, I also realize, regardless of my not-so-fabulous plan, that he has been the one to ask me out this whole time. Being my wingman for dinner at P.F. Chang's doesn't count.

"Do you want to do something? When you get back?" I rush the words out, frantically trying to come up with something we could do together. All I really want to do is kick Duff out again, but that's not an option. Although I think he may be gone for a few days anyway.

"Yes." Tobias breathes the word out. "I'll call you when I land? Or when I get home and have my phone again."

"Okay. I, uh, I can't wait to see you." I flush hot, even though Carly has gone back upstairs and no one else is around to hear my words.

"Me too," Tobias replies.

TWENTY-SEVEN

Chapter Twenty-Seven—Tobias

SARAH-MICHELLE: Dad   is   pissed   off.
Congratulations!

I roll my eyes toward the ceiling, where garish chandeliers hang over our heads. I've been trying to calculate how much they weigh. My sister has found out, probably through Rowan, that I'm in Vegas with Charley, and now she's using his number to send me messages. I'm lurking in the back of a banquet room listening to a discussion about environmental geology, of which I understand about every third word. Charley and his client are sitting together at the front of the room.

Charley's ex, Simon Ellison, sits two rows behind them, a scowl on his handsome face. Simon is hot. Like, even *I* think he's hot, and he is not my type. Simon puts the "jock" in "rocks for jocks." He should be illegal. And, for whatever reason, the scowl he's sporting makes him seem hotter. But he's also an asshole who turned Charley into a cynical jerk (except to me, of course), and my job is to have Charley's back for the weekend.

I turn my attention back to Charley's cell phone, which I have in case Simon texts him. Simon has done no such thing; I don't know if he's noticed me back here or if he'd recognize me.

TOBIAS: GOOD. MAYBE HE'LL BELIEVE ME NOW. I'M GOING TO GIVE MY NOTICE.

Although, the thought strikes me, now that Arnie works there... maybe I should hold off. Maybe it won't be so bad if I have an ally?

I can't believe how long it took me to figure out how to contact Arnie. I owe Carly a month's worth of iced lattes for doing me a personal favor. The instant I heard Arnie's voice, I *knew* he was upset. He probably spent yesterday making up all kinds of ridiculous scenarios about us—see, I do know him that well.

I'd spent yesterday evening making excuses to Charley's client about food poisoning and holding his hair away from his face as he rid himself of the tremendous amount of alcohol he'd sucked down while waiting for my plane to land. I love Charley —he's my best friend—but I'm starting to think maybe he's not over Simon.

SARAH-MICHELLE: IF THAT'S WHAT YOU WANT TO DO. HOPEFULLY DAD WONT FIRE YOU FIRST.

TOBIAS: NO, HE'S DECIDED I FIT A DEMOGRAPHIC.

SARAH-MICHELLE: HE'S JUST MAD AT YOU BECAUSE MOM FINALLY FIGURED OUT HE'S HAVING AN AFFAIR.

He is? How did I not know that? Subtle is not Andrew Barrington's middle name.

TOBIAS: HE IS? HOW DO YOU KNOW?

SARAH-MICHELLE: GOD, SOMETIMES YOU ARE SO OBLIV-IOUS. ITS BEEN GOING ON FOR AGES. AND I KNOW BECAUSE UNLIKE YOU I PAY ATTENTION.

That stings. I pay attention, don't I? Just in case she's right, I look around the room again and notice Simon has disappeared. Maybe Sarah-Michelle has a point.

Tobias: Who is it?

Sarah-Michelle: Im not sure yet maybe someone from work *gag face emoji*

Tobias: Almost a year? And mom is just figuring it out?

Sarah-Michelle: You picked a great time to run away from home big brother.

We chat for a little while longer while I try to digest the fact that my father is having an affair. I'm honestly not surprised. It's not as if I believe my parents' marriage is particularly happy. The two of them seem more like foreign countries in a constant state of trade negotiation than two people in a committed relationship.

THE CONFERENCE BREAKS for the day, which is good, since I can't handle much more. I'm bored out of my mind; rocks are not my thing. But I figure by the end of Saturday evening I'll be in the black with Charley—he may even owe me.

"I'm taking myself sightseeing," I tell him when we're upstairs in our hotel room at the Bellagio. I want to check out all the places in Las Vegas where big movies have been filmed. While I was guarding Charley, I made a list. I'm going to try and catch a plane home tomorrow, so all my sightseeing needs to be tonight.

Charley glances over at me. He's changing clothes. He and his client are headed out to dinner; later there's some sort of geological event. I ask Charley if there's a rock band, but he doesn't bother to answer me; he merely slays me with a glance that would melt... rock. Charley looks nice in a pair of light linen slacks and a casual cotton shirt the same shade of blue as his eyes, finished off with leather sandals. He always looks nice. Even if he does have dark circles under his eyes.

"Take my phone with you," he says.

I shake my head. "You aren't going to need me tonight." Charley's got a dinner with his client, and they might go dancing afterward, but unless Simon Ellison has managed to stash a GPS somewhere on Charley, he won't be there.

"Take it anyway. And don't turn it off. That way if I do need you, I can call you."

"Fine." I take the thing and tuck it into the pocket of my shorts. "Are you going to tell me why you thought it was a good idea to attend a conference entirely devoted to geology?"

"Stupidity."

"Charley, as your best friend, if I know one thing about you, it's this: you're anything but stupid."

"Yeah, well, I didn't see this coming, okay?" He gazes at me. I see an emotion in his eyes he usually hides or laughs off: hurt. I could kill Simon Ellison for what he's done.

After being inside the hotel all day, the heat of Vegas feels like a slap in the face, although the concierge I stopped to ask directions from claims it's cooled off already. The famous Bellagio fountains turn off just as I exit the lobby, but they'll be on again in a half hour. I'll get a chance to see them later. *Ocean's Eleven*—a movie I adore—was filmed here at the Bellagio, and I wish, not for the first time, Arnie were here with me so we could talk about it and discover the city together.

As I'm trying to decide which direction to head in, an idea strikes me. I spend a few minutes using Charley's phone to search the places I want to see tonight. If I'm an aspiring filmmaker, I might as well start now. I dash back inside the hotel and search out the gift shop, and, sure enough—it is the Bellagio after all—they sell portable battery packs and charging cables. I'm good to go.

Tobias: What are you doing?

Arnie: ...um, watching a show. Having popcorn for dinner. The usual hijinks.

Tobias: Is it going to bug you if I send you a bunch of videos and stuff? I thought we could go on a virtual date...

Almost immediately the phone vibrates in my hand. Grinning like a fool, I answer. "Hey."

"Hey," repeats Arnie, "I'd love to go on a virtual date. I've never been to Las Vegas. What are we going to do?"

"We're going to check out all the places I can get to tonight where famous movies were filmed. We'll start here, I mean at the Bellagio, where I am now."

"*Ocean's Eleven*—I love all those movies!"

"Me too," I respond. "Me too." I'm pretty sure I love Arnie Ferguson too, but I can't say that yet.

The first thing I do is make my way through the foot traffic to Las Vegas Boulevard. With the fountains behind me, I take a selfie and send it to Arnie.

We spend the next four hours talking and texting each other. By ten I'm wiped out. I've walked miles, snapping selfies and recording quick takes at various locations. The battery pack indicator is flashing orange—I've managed to deplete it.

We've been to the Mirage, where part of *Vegas Vacation* was filmed—ah, the Griswold family. I've walked up and down the Strip while I tried to find specific locations in *Leaving Las Vegas*. Arnie hasn't seen it, but I have.

After getting turned around, which is remarkably easy in this town with all its neon lights, I stop for a minute and a hawker hands me a pamphlet. You would not believe how many people try to give you stuff here. I start to tell him I'm not interested in naked women when I realize it's a coupon for something called Axe Monkeys.

"Oh my god, Arnie, we can go axe throwing! I legitimately did not know this was a thing!"

"Axe throwing? I think there's a place on, or near, Broadway. I've never been. It seems like one of those things I'd do to get aggression out. Maybe. I bet I'd be terrible at it."

"I kinda think you can be bad at axe throwing these days. Maybe our ancestors had to be good, though?"

"I'm pretty sure my ancestors did the smart thing and hid," Arnie replies.

Maybe I should take Charley. He probably has aggressions to get out. I shove the slip of paper into my pocket. You just never know.

Caesars Palace is on the way back to the Bellagio. I stop and take a selfie in the garish lobby; it's so over the top I have to squint not to be overwhelmed. Vegas in general is over the top, way more than I expected it to be. Which is sort of ridiculous. I've seen all the movies, after all.

After sending the photo to Arnie, I call him again, pausing in front of the famous fountains as they come on. "I'm heading back upstairs. I just wanted to say good night." I'm not talking to Arnie on the phone with Charley in the room.

"This has been so much fun, way better than a Netflix binge. The only thing that would have made our date better is if I was there with you. Thank you, Tobias. I, uh, can't wait to see you."

I love it when Arnie gets all shy. I'm shy too, so I understand. "Me either." My response is quiet. There is so much more I want to say, but not over the phone.

Hands down, this has been the best date of my life. A hopeful feeling is blooming. I think things are only going to get better between Arnie and me.

As I'm waiting for the elevator, I chuckle to myself. Who would've thought Arnie and I would find each other again after all these years? The only identifying feature I'd remembered from the night of the party was his Australia-shaped birthmark. Stopping at the Buzz all those weeks ago feels like fate intervening on our behalf. I swear, I don't believe in that kind of stuff, but a secret part of me thinks we're meant to be together... and I will do whatever I need to to make it happen.

Chapter Twenty-Eight—Arnie

I'M HOPING Tobias will get home Saturday, but he doesn't know yet if "the Charley situation" will let him escape before Sunday. So, when my mom calls that morning, there's no excuse I can use to wiggle out of the dinner with her at the dentist's house. I have to meet *them* alone.

Which I totally can do. I'm embracing this change thing.

Mom retrieves me late Saturday afternoon. Considering her driving is as bad as Tobias's, it says something about my level of distraction and lack of self-preservation that I accept her offer to pick me up—although a bus to Edmonds would take forever. Maybe I should have taken the bus after all, though.

I hardly cringe when she's tailing someone in the carpool lane before getting impatient and zipping past the person (who is driving the speed limit, I note) on the right. "Mom, it's not a race," I remark in what I feel is a perfectly reasonable tone. I don't think the dentist is going to start the barbecue without her. Maybe without me, but not without Mom.

She ignores me. I sigh.

I'm so glad my mom has found someone. I really am. I'm just not good at sharing her. I've had her to myself for years, even before the divorce. As this thought crosses my mind, kind of expanding and taking over like a thought fog, I realize how selfish I've been. I owe her to meet Will's daughters and try to get to know them. Like them or not, there are going to be more events like this one in the future. And then there will be the wedding itself. Just because I don't exactly embrace change doesn't make it stop happening.

"We're here!" she announces.

Will lives in Edmonds, about twenty miles north of Seattle. It's a cute town right on Puget Sound with a community theater, little shops, and some nice restaurants. There's also a ferry terminal; at the wrong time, traffic can be a bitch. Mom pulls to the curb on a street of newer, two-tone townhouses. I'm looking up and down the block trying to figure out which one is Will's when the nearest front door opens and he appears, waving and smiling at us. At my mother specifically, I figure, but I plaster my best smile on and even wave back. I can do this, I tell myself.

"Don't worry, they'll love you," my mom says as we get out of the car.

Moms only say those kinds of things when they know their kids are worried. I don't always make the best impression—and I already have a feeling of doom about this "little get-together," but I shove it away. I like to think I grow on people, but seeing as my own father chose a whole new family that didn't include me, I guess I'm not convinced. For my mom I am going to do my best.

"Thanks for coming," Will says as he shakes my hand.

"Thanks for having me."

"Hopefully we'll be having a lot more of these get-togethers," he says enthusiastically. "Come on in. I'd like to introduce you to Alex and Jo."

I follow him through the front room, not even noticing the décor, and into the kitchen at the back of the house, where a sliding door leads out to a patio and fenced yard that has beds filled with late-blooming flowers. Two young women are standing outside, talking animatedly.

For a minute I'm stricken. My feet turn to lead. What am I'm going to say? I stop walking, but my mom pokes me between the shoulder blades. Taking her hint, I step across the sill. I wish Tobias were here; he's so much better at these situations than I am.

Okay, I've only been in the one other situation like this with him, but he was a rock star.

Will's daughters turn toward us in tandem as the screen door slides open. They're nearly identical. They look like their dad: dark hair, wide dark eyes, and perfect bright white smiles. Perks of having a dentist for a dad, I suppose. They're sporty. I can tell already by their running shoes and track pants. I am not sporty. I'm a gold medalist in solo events like reading and walking. And I've been known to read and walk at the same time, which did not turn out well for me.

We regard each other warily. I have the absurd idea that the three of us are much like strange cats being introduced to each other, my mom and Will watching closely to see if we'll be able to coexist. Will the lionesses attack or leave the interloper alone? I take a mental deep breath and channel my best Tobias. All I need to do is be nice.

"Would you like a glass of wine?" Will offers.

Screw my mental Tobias; bring the whole bottle over here, please.

Will must understand the expression on my face, because

he immediately turns and goes back inside, returning moments later with a bottle of wine and a bottle opener. I gratefully accept a glass of chardonnay. Thank god for alcohol.

"Arnie, this is Alex," Will indicates the slightly taller girl, "and this is Jo. Come on over, girls, and meet your..." He pauses. "Arnie."

I shut my eyes and try not to gulp down the excellent wine all at once, but I have a sneaking suspicion I'm going to need more than one glass.

Poor Will. But his flub does the trick. At least the three of us can look at each other now, and I think they might be as uncomfortable as I am. Except of course they're sisters and already know each other.

"Hi," I offer.

"Hi," the sisters say.

"Uh, hey, so your dad, my mom." *Stop*, I scream in my head, and about another inch of wine goes down the hatch. Jo—I think; now that I'm closer they seem to be the same height—snickers. My mom says, "Let's go figure out this chicken, Will," in a super unsneaky attempt to leave us alone.

Remarkably, they are nice. I don't know why I find this shocking. I guess I'm conditioned to people thinking I'm weird. It takes only a few minutes for the three of us to figure out we all are a bit shocked by our parents' upcoming marriage. Also, Alex is a huge *Doctor Who* fan, and (surprise) so am I. The verdict is out on the best Doctor, but the connection is there.

Jo is quieter than her sister, but when we start talking Seattle sports teams (because even though I'm not a hockey fan, I do want a Seattle Kraken jersey) she pipes up about the men's soccer team and how they pale in comparison to the women.

"Do you play?" I ask.

"I played in high school, but not so much anymore."

"Don't let her fool you," says Alex. "Jo played on all the elite teams and was even offered a scholarship."

"That's cool. I'm so uncoordinated I can't even play hacky-sack."

"You actually have to be pretty coordinated to play hacky-sack," Jo says seriously.

"I mean, I have no skills."

"I bet you do," she insists.

And this is how I find myself playing a semi-tipsy game of "See if Alex or Arnie can score off Jo." A well-used soccer net sits at the back of Will's yard, and the three of us kick the ball around until Will calls us over for dinner. I prove I was right; I have no skills. But it's okay because I think I made some friends.

"I THINK THAT WENT WELL, don't you?" Mom comments as we pull away from the curb.

I'm willing to admit things went well. Possibly a tad better: Will's daughters and I aren't mortal enemies; we might even manage to become friends. "It did. Alex and Jo seem nice."

I surreptitiously check my phone to see if I have a text from Tobias. Nothing yet. I resign myself to not seeing him until tomorrow.

"This is a big change for them as well. They've had Will to themselves for a long time."

"They like you, Mom. As long as you're happy, we'll all be fine."

"Who are you, and what have you done with Arnie?"

"Ha ha, Mom. This is me," I swept my hand down the front of my body, "your favorite son, accepting change into his life."

We both laugh. Then I stop talking because I want Mom to concentrate on the road. And her driving *hasn't* changed.

Late-evening traffic back into Seattle is light. I rest my head against the headrest, watching the other cars go by. Mom is quiet for a mile or so, which makes me nervous. I brace myself for whatever is coming next.

"I know this has been a lot for you, but I want you to know I'm proud of you."

"Thanks, Mom, I think it's called acting like an adult."

She giggles. "I guess. Although being an adult is overrated. Do you remember being frustrated that all the mail came with my name or your father's name and you wanted your own mail?"

"I don't, but it sounds like me."

"I told you you'd get plenty of mail when you were an adult. You got so angry, you accused me of using a bad word. It still makes me laugh."

"I'm glad I continue to provide amusement for you." But I laugh too, because I'm pretty sure I still think "adult" is a bad word.

"Do you think you and Will's girls will get along?"

I can tell by Mom's tone that this is something she's been worrying about. I twist around in my seat so I can see her better.

"We're adults, as you pointed out. I think things will be fine. I mean, I don't know if they'll be my best friends. But we'll figure it out."

MY APARTMENT FEELS QUIET. Usually I like the quiet, but tonight I wish Duff were home. He flew to Monterey yesterday for a shoot and won't be back for a week or something like that. Stripping out of my meet-the-family attire, I flop onto my futon in only my boxers. Hey, a boy can mope if he wants to.

I'm not really moping, though. A thrum of excitement hums

just underneath my skin. No matter what, I will see Tobias tomorrow, and we get to start again. I mean, really being together. Or trying, anyway. I have this fear I'm going to mess everything up. If I want something too much, it goes away.

Sleep sneaks up on me. I'm having a weird dream about being in a play (I've never been in a play, so this is a surprise in itself). I've forgotten my lines, and I'm wandering around the stage just hoping I'm doing the right thing. There's an actor offstage who's trying to get my attention: tap, tap, tap... Why is he knocking?

I flail awake. Someone is tapping on my door.

Of course it's Tobias. I knew it would be before I flung open the door—who else would be tapping? Later I will wonder how he got past the building's stellar (not) security, but for right now all I can do is stare at him with my mouth hanging wide open.

"Hi," he says. "I hope this is okay."

"Is this okay?" I squeak, looking down at myself, belatedly realizing I've opened my door wearing only my underwear. This doesn't seem to bother Tobias, who is looking at me as if I'm freshly baked bread and he's been on a low-carb diet for months. Me too. I mean, that's how I'm looking back at him.

"I should've texted, but I didn't even stop at my house to get my phone. For one thing, my sister is probably lying in wait, and for another, I'd probably have to talk to my father—or at least read or listen to the messages he's sure to have left on my phone. So I came straight here."

Tobias is rambling on about things he should've done to make up for being irresponsible, but instead he came here. To see me. Because he wanted to. See me.

Me. Arnie Ferguson.

I bolt into action, grabbing Tobias's arm and dragging him across the threshold. I do not need Mr. Garrison from down the hall to decide he needs to check the noise in the hallway. He's a nice old man, but he'd take one look at Tobias and I'd never get rid of him. He definitely has an eye for the younger guys, but he's tired of ogling me and Duff.

Well, maybe just me. Most people don't seem to tire of ogling my roommate.

With Tobias inside and the door shut, the apartment seems much smaller than usual, and suddenly I'm at a loss for words. (Right, how did that happen?) Plus I remember I'm in my underwear, and while I've watched that scene in *Risky Business* a million times (I was fifteen; I give myself a break), I do not wear them as sexily as what's-his-name.

It doesn't matter, though. Tobias steps out of the flip-flops he's wearing and moves right into my space. His pupils are huge, and he still has that hungry expression. "So, this really is okay?"

I nod, looking up into his eyes. "Yes, this is really okay."

A shy smile flits across his face. "I stopped at the 24-hour Bartell for supplies."

He's close enough to me now that he whispers this into my ear, and my entire body is immediately engulfed in a wave of lust. I do the only logical thing I can do: I close the distance between us and kiss him.

Tobias is enough taller than me that I have to stand on my toes, my hands cupping his face. At first we're just kissing, like our lips are reacquainting themselves, but then Tobias wraps his arms around me and crushes me against him. I can feel everything, including his erection trapped in his shorts. He has far too many clothes on, which I intend to rectify.

I try to keep my lips on his as I reach between us to unfasten his shorts, but all I do is knock my forehead into his chin.

"Are you okay?" I ask as I keep fumbling with the button. "Were these designed with a childproof snap?" I grumble. "Everyone knows only kids can get into those things."

Tobias steps away, and I'm immediately chilled. Luckily he

seems to know how to get himself undressed, and his linen cargo-style shorts fall to the floor to pool around his feet. He's wearing white boxer briefs that hug his package in the most delicious way.

I allow myself to enjoy the sight for about a half second before slipping my fingers underneath the elastic band and tugging them downward. His cock pops out of its confinement and points directly at me.

And yes, that is exactly what I want. Dropping to my knees (which looks way easier in porn, thank you very much), I grab the base and flick my tongue out to taste him, licking his tip. Tobias groans. I look up but don't stop what I'm doing. He's stopped unbuttoning his shirt and instead is watching me. I feel him pulse a little against my lip and in my hand. It's amazing. I love this feeling. It's a heady power, knowing I'm the one making him feel this way.

"Arnie..."

"Mmm?" I answer with my mouth full of him.

"Arnie," he tries again.

I want to say, "That's my name, don't wear it out," but instead, like a mature adult with a cock in my mouth, I suck him harder. If he can form thoughts into words, I'm not doing it right. I have no gag reflex; this is something I learned about myself while practicing with various fruits in order to be ready for this very moment. Opening my jaw wider, I take him all the way down.

He flails around, and finally his hands land on my head. I like having them there, like I'm knocking him off his feet and he needs help to stay upright. His fingers wind through my hair—which is not as long as I like, due to the new job. One of my hands is grabbing his ass, and I use the other to massage his balls, which are already pulled up and ready to go. I trace the line between his sac and his entrance, and Tobias moans and gives up not canting into my mouth. I smile.

One of his hands leaves my head. He reaches around and caresses my neck, where, no doubt, he can feel the head of his penis inside my throat. We both groan. I'm so hard it hurts, but I can't touch myself. My hands are full, so to speak. I'm wondering if I'll be able to come with no friction.

As I'm thinking that, I push my finger a little further back so I'm touching his hole. I trace around it, wanting more. I will have Tobias in my ass before the night is through; this is just the beginning. Tobias clenches. I know he's going to come. His balls are rocks, and my cock is doing its best to break out of its cotton prison, my boxers wet from precome. There's this moment that hangs in time just before Tobias releases, and then I taste him, swallowing as much as I can as he spills into my mouth and down my throat.

My own erection throbs painfully. Pulling off Tobias, I reach down to get myself off. I'm twenty-four; I'll be ready again later.

"No." Tobias manages to pull his half-unbuttoned shirt off over his head, throwing it next to his shorts.

"No?" I repeat.

"Get on the bed, on your back."

I don't even bother to stand up; I crawl the three feet to my futon and collapse onto my back. Tobias stares at me, his semi-flaccid cock listing a little to the left. He is gorgeous. His thighs alone are sexy, sprinkled with the dark hair that begins at his groin.

He doesn't let me look long, though. In seconds he's kneeling over me, palming my cock through my boxers, and my erection, which had subsided the tiniest amount, rages back. "What do you want?"

"I don't care. I just want to come." I'm begging, and he hasn't even been touching me for twenty seconds. I arch up against his hand. It isn't going to take much.

After tugging my briefs down and flinging them aside (I think they land on my side table), he sits back on his haunches and looks at me. For once, I'm not shy. I know Tobias likes what he sees. And no, this isn't our first or our second time, but—it's the real time. My dick is engorged, and as we watch, a small amount of precome pulses from it. Tobias leans down and licks me. His tongue is hot, wet and soft, but I want his mouth.

"Please," I gibber.

The smile on his face is not nice at all. I suspect he's going to try and draw this out. I don't know if I will be able to make it. Spoiler alert: I don't.

The millisecond Tobias sucks my throbbing cock into his mouth, I am done. I fight it, but blowing Tobias had been too much, too arousing, too everything. Sparks—damn, police flares —run up my spine, unstoppable. I'm writhing on the mattress, my hips moving back and forth without my permission. Sweat runs down the side of my face; I'm burning up. He runs the tip of his tongue around my head, tracing underneath the cap where, *note*, I am incredibly sensitive—and that's the last straw.

"Oh, shit," I say, because I'm extra romantic when it comes to pillow talk, "oh shit, oh shit."

My balls seize, and I'm coming. I come so hard I forget to breathe for a minute and get lightheaded. Tobias does his best, but there is come everywhere. I pulse into his mouth, and it dribbles back out onto my stomach. He lets me slip out of his mouth, and that's such a hot image more come streams onto my stomach, adding to what's already there.

Tobias slumps against my side while I try to get my world to right itself.

"That was incredible," he says.

I nod, because I still can't form words.

But suddenly I can. "I still want you to fuck me."

Tobias groans, and in the dim light I see his cock twitch, totally on board with the idea.

Chapter Twenty-Nine—Tobias

WE TAKE A SHOWER TOGETHER, making sure all the important places are clean, and start over. We're back on the bed, Arnie on his knees in front of me with his ass in the air. It's probably a good thing we got off earlier; one glimpse at Arnie's hole and I'm hard again. Supposedly assholes aren't supposed to be sexy, but no one told my libido that.

I kind of want to lick him, but I've never done that before.

Arnie grumbles, "Jesus Christ, get to it."

I chuckle, but I'm impatient too, so I "get to it."

The lube and condoms I brought are on the floor next to the bed. I grab the lube and squirt some onto my fingers, then I spread his cheeks and dribble some there too.

"Fuck, that's cold."

"You told me to get to it."

"I did."

First I rub the lube around his hole with one finger; then,

when he's moaning and pushing backward, seeking more, I use both my thumbs and tease him, pushing one in, then the other, then both and back to one again, loosening him and also setting myself on fire.

We both came like an hour ago, and I'm so hard already it's as if it never happened. All I want is to feel Arnie's tight heat around my dick. I slip two fingers inside him, entranced by the way his hole flexes around my fingers. My cock is dripping onto the sheets. I reach between Arnie's legs to make sure he's doing okay. His erection is hot and heavy in my hand. I pump him once, and he groans and tries to rub himself against me.

No way. When Arnie comes, I want to be inside him. I pull my hand away, and he whimpers. As quickly as I can, I roll on a condom. Then I'm holding my cock and pushing the tip of it against Arnie's hole, asking to be let past the gates.

"Relax." With one hand, I rub the small of his back. His hole opens, and I slide past that first muscle into his heat. "Oh, fuck," I whisper.

Arnie feels incredible—better than I'd imagined, and I've imagined an awful lot over the past few weeks. He clenches and relaxes around me. It's intense and better than anything I've felt before. I push farther in, and his entire body jolts. I wish we were doing this bareback, because I want to feel my come inside him. I need to stop thinking about this. I'm losing control. Arnie spreads his knees farther apart, his back arched at an impossible angle, and now I do lose control. I pound into him, sliding back and forth against his prostate, and he's giving himself to me, helplessly begging for more, open wide. No doubt the neighbors are getting a show tonight. I caress his hole with my index finger, loving how he's open and wide around my cock. My cock. No anyone else's. Mine.

"You are mine, Arnie Ferguson."

"Yes, oh god fuck yes, god, I am yours." He tightens around me. I reach between his legs again, because I want to feel him on my dick *and* against my hand—I'm a greedy guy, I guess. I pump him once or twice, and he's coming: clenching, shouting, and groaning as his orgasm hits him. Come streams through my fingers as he grinds against me, and his asshole squeezes my cock in a final spasm of electricity.

I'm coming too. I couldn't stop myself if I wanted to—which I do not. The condom fills with my release. I think I groan or shout, but I don't know. All I know is, the lightning sparks in my balls and lights me up from the inside out. When I open my eyes again, I'm slumped over Arnie's back, my still-mostly-hard cock jammed in his ass like it's found its home.

Holding on to the condom, I gently pull out and ditch it at the side of the bed.

Arnie is still lying on his stomach. I lie down next to him and stroke the map of his spine with my fingers. He's a bit sweaty, and his shoulder twitches as if my touch tickles.

"Iakjshr la," is what I think he says.

"Sorry?"

He turns his head so he's facing me. His eyes are half-shut; his hair is smashed down on the side and sticking straight up on the top. He's gorgeous. My heart thumps.

"I think I had an out-of-body experience," he mumbles.

"Oh, no, that was definitely an in-the-body experience."

Arnie lifts his head enough to stare at me and shake his head before chuckling. "A Tobias-body experience."

"It was okay?" I hate being nervous about sex.

"It was incredible. Come 'ere."

Arnie rolls onto his side, lifting up one arm and inviting me to move closer.

"One sec. I'm going to grab a washcloth."

Minutes later I've wiped the come off Arnie's abs and placed a towel between him and the spunk-covered sheets. Personally, I'm not a fan of waking up sticky and smelling like come. But maybe if it was Arnie's? It's a possibility.

"Thank you," he murmurs. "It's nice having you take care of me."

I realize with a jolt—more shocking than the moment I realized I am irrevocably in love with him—I want to take care of Arnie. I want all the things. I want to hold hands, make dinner together, bicker about who took the trash out last. I want to be with him, forever. With a grunt, I tuck myself around him, very much feeling like I need to be the big spoon right now. Maybe not always, but in this moment, I need to hold him. I guess that's what love is.

"SURE," Arnie agrees. "The worst your dad can do is fire me. And I happen to have another couple interviews lined up this week."

"Really?" I ask, looking at him with his tousled hair and sleepy eyes. "You're not just saying that to make me feel better?"

We woke late, our legs tangled together and hands touching like we couldn't bring ourselves to separate even in sleep. I have to go home and face the music, even though all I want to do is feel Arnie's body against mine again. My morning wood is demanding attention, but I have to ignore it. This time.

"I'm not kidding about the interviews, and remember, you went to dinner with my mom and her dentist-man—Will— before we were even really together."

Arnie is right, but I have a feeling meeting my parents is going to be a lot different from meeting Rita and Will. For one thing, Rita and, by proxy, Will, cares about her son. She's involved in his life; she's rooting for him to succeed in his own way. Miles apart from my experience.

After showering and getting off together anyway—at least the day won't be a complete waste—we decide to walk to my parents' house. It's about two miles, and the morning is cool and dewy. Fall is definitely on the way. We hold hands the entire time, and random things catch my eye: a single red-green leaf on a maple tree, late-blooming daisies, Arnie's secret mischievous smile when he thinks I'm not paying attention. I've left my bag at his place—Arnie is "pretty sure" Duff won't be home for a few days, which is the best news I've heard in a while, and it's been a pretty awesome morning so far.

About the moment we turn the final corner and the house I grew up in is just a block or so away, I remember my conversation with Sarah-Michelle about my parents: that my dad has been having an affair and my mother only just found out. I was too busy thinking about Arnie to worry about them, and besides, a part of me doesn't give a damn.

I remember now because my father is standing on the front lawn shouting, while my mother, in a very *Down by Law* (only with more money) scene, hurls his belongings out the window of their second-story bedroom. In the distance I hear the faint sound of a police siren, and it's getting closer and louder. With a sinking heart, I think I know their destination.

"What do you want to do?" Arnie asks me. "We could turn around and pretend like we never saw a thing. Honestly, I have no idea what the protocol is in a situation like this. What is even happening? And..." He glances back at the action. "Does your mom like that movie too, the one you took me to?"

A grim chuckle escapes me. Arnie is smart and observant.

I'm curious how Olivia lured Andrew outside this morning. But maybe, like me, he's been gone all night and only now returning.

"Is there something I should know?" Arnie whispers as the siren gets closer and closer. I notice a little crowd of neighbors down the street. This must have been going on for a while if people on my street have actually ventured outside to get a better view. On the other hand, maybe they're eager to see the downfall of the great and arrogant Andrew Barrington.

"Sarah-Michelle told me my mother found out Andrew is having an affair, but I forgot," I mutter, desperately wishing I didn't have to think about it now. "It makes me sound like a terrible person, but in my defense, my attention was on you these past few days." I shrug. There isn't anything else I can say, and it's not my job to clean up their messes anyhow.

We stand there for a minute, watching. My mother comes back to the balcony with an armful of clothing—my dad's beloved business suits—and heaves the whole thing over the railing. A pair of slacks snags on a flower box and dangles by the hem of one pant leg, a sort of grotesque effigy.

I'm impressed Olivia has managed to lock him outside, but then I realize, with the staff gone for the day, Andrew can't demand they let him in. Where is my sister?

As if my thought summoned her, Sarah-Michelle's voice floats from behind us. "You picked a great morning to come home!" Turning around, I spot her and Rowan Hunter standing together on the Hunters' side porch on the other side of the street. From there they have an unimpeded view of the goings-on at our house.

"Sarah-Michelle! What happened?" I drag Arnie across the street with me; I am not letting go of him right now.

The Hunters' house squats on the corner and is bigger, older, and much prettier than ours. The parcel is something like 15,000 square feet, unheard of in Seattle these days. The side porch is big enough to hold a bench-style porch swing as well as a table and chairs, and it has a ceiling fan—which is handy about two weeks out of the year, but it does look pretty. Arnie and I jog up the steps to join Rowan and Sarah-Michelle.

"Spill," I demand once I'm close enough I don't have to yell.

"Sit down," Rowan says. "Do you want some coffee?" I like Rowan. She's a lot like her brother, although you wouldn't know it by looking at them. Somewhere in her family genes dark hair and blue eyes linger, but she has Charley's sense of humor, and even if she and Sarah-Michelle aren't besties, Rowan is a good friend.

Arnie answers her question. "I don't know about Tobias, but *I* want coffee. Thank you..."

"Oh, crap. Arnie, this is my sister, Sarah-Michelle, and Charley's sister, Rowan. And this"—I tug Arnie closer to me—"is my boyfriend, Arnie Ferguson." Arnie flushes a bright red, but I don't miss the pleased expression that flits across his face as he squeezes my hand and presses hard against my side.

"Great to meet you, Arnie. I'm going to grab some coffee." Rowan disappears inside.

Sarah-Michelle steps forward. I think she's going to shake Arnie's hand, but instead she grabs him in a full-body hug before declaring, "I'm so glad to finally meet you!" Arnie looks stunned and pleased and flustered all at once.

I can't help but kiss him. I'm aiming for his forehead, but he moves and instead I smooch the corner of his eye. He squints at me. "What was that for?" I shrug and smile. It's because I love him, but I can't tell him that yet. Sarah-Michelle grins at me like she knows my secret. She probably does, because she's smart like that.

THERE'S ANOTHER SHOUT, and we all turn back in the direction of my parents and the drama that's playing out in front of the entire neighborhood. The slacks are still dangling. Olivia has something shiny in her hand now, and her arm is cocked back, ready to release it. My dad has his hands up, imploring her to stop, to let him inside so they can talk about it. I notice none of the words he utters include "I'm sorry."

The police car rolls up to the curb and turns its siren off. We are in old Seattle; the streets are narrow, and the officer has to stop in the traffic lane and leave her lights flashing as she gets out of the cruiser. My dad turns to say something to her, and my mother retreats inside and bangs the French doors shut behind her. Sarah-Michelle and I both sigh.

"Who is it, do you know?" I ask. "That he's having the affair with, I mean." I've never seen my mother show this much emotion.

Sarah-Michelle sits down on the porch swing and stares at me, her eyes wide. "It's his assistant, Carly." She whispers the name as if our mother can hear from where she is holed up inside the house.

"I knew it," Arnie exclaims. "I knew I recognized her—or at least her back. Or something. I just couldn't figure out where from!"

We're both staring at him now. He grins and shrugs. "Back when I was plotting—uh, finding out more about you—I found pictures online of your father and Carly together. They're all from the back, but it's definitely her."

I shake my head. "Remind me never to do something I don't want you to find out."

Rowan comes back outside carrying a tray holding four mugs and a carafe with a matching sugar-and-cream set. She sets the tray on the table, and we all help ourselves to coffee. Arnie and I sit together at the table while Rowan and Sarah-Michelle claim the swing, gently moving forward and back as they sip their drinks.

As we're spying, the responding officer knocks on our front

door. It opens, and she and my mom talk in the doorway for a few minutes. Then Olivia opens the door wider and lets the officer inside while my dad waits on the sidewalk with the other officer, fuming. I'm watching him for some sign he regrets what's happened, but I'm pretty sure he only regrets being caught.

"So... Carly? Really? I thought she was smarter than that." I'm disappointed.

"My dad left my mom for his secretary," Arnie says.

"Oh yeah?" I don't know much about Arnie's dad; he's only told me they aren't close.

"I think they were over before that, but the affair was the final nail in the coffin of their relationship, so to speak."

We're all quiet for a few minutes, waiting to see if the public drama is over for the time being.

"For a long time, I thought the divorce was my fault. My father... doesn't really accept me. Not because of the gay thing, that was just icing on the cake, but he wanted me to be a 'real' boy." Arnie grimaces. "To play softball and be on the swim team, because that's what *he* did. But I don't like that kind of competition, and games and meets always stressed me out. I loved gymnastics, but he hated it—too girlie. One time after T-ball, he asked me what I learned (we'd lost, of course), and I told him I learned it takes seven innings for a spider to spin a web. I didn't care about the ball; I wanted to be on the bench watching the spider. He got mad and yelled at me, and of course I cried, which boys don't do. Anyway, it took me a while to understand that was all on him. And now I've totally overshared."

I wrap my arm around his waist and tug him even closer. I don't ever want to meet Arnie's father.

On the one hand, the introductions I'd been nervous about won't be happening today, but on the other, I need my phone, and it's in my bedroom. My best bet is probably to get it now. I hope. "I'm going to go around back and grab my phone."

"Good luck."

I look at my sister. "Why?"

"She spent the last couple of days having every single lock in the house changed. Your keys are no good."

"What... Where was Andrew?" I ask her.

"Supposedly on a business trip."

"Do you have a key?"

Grinning, Sarah-Michelle reaches into the pocket of her hoodie and pulls out her keys. The goofy Pokémon figure I gave her years ago still dangles from the ring. She tosses them to me.

THE POLICE OFFICER convinces Olivia to allow my father inside to pack some of his belongings as long as someone is with him to make sure he doesn't take anything not his. By this time my mother's lawyer has arrived. *Words* are being tossed around, but my mother stands firm. She and Andrew are over; Carly was the last straw. I also learn my mother has considerable money of her own, and even after twenty-six years of marriage my father doesn't have access to it. In fact, I learn my mother has been bankrolling Barrington Properties for years. I had no idea; my stomach roils as I wonder what is going to happen with the business. I don't want to work there, but a lot of people depend on Barrington for their salary. Including Arnie.

I try to get Arnie go home, but he insists he'll wait with Sarah-Michelle and Rowan.

"I'll just hang out here and see if I can pump your sister for information about you," he says with an impish grin. All three of them laugh evilly, and I roll my eyes, because obviously this is a battle I am not going to win.

Attempting to blend in with the landscaping, I creep across

the street and around the side of the house. Andrew has been escorted inside by the lawyer; my mother is nowhere in sight. The police turn off their flashers and are slowly leaving. The neighbors, sensing the end of today's drama, are drifting back inside their homes.

As I'm sneaking down the back stairs with my phone in my possession, trying to avoid the one squeaky stair as if I've been out all night—well, I have, but I'm twenty-four and being out all night is no big deal—I come face to face with my mother. I stop, open my mouth, and shut it again, because I don't know what to say to her. Is there a Hallmark card for this situation?

"Hi, Olivia. Uh, grabbing my phone." I wave it at her as if she needs proof.

"Tobias." She looks up at me; I'm kind of looming two steps above her. "I suppose you know about your father?"

I vaguely wave toward the Hunters'. "Sarah-Michelle told me. She and Rowan are across the street."

"Ah."

"I, um, was bringing Arnie by to meet you, but I think we'll save it for another time."

"Probably a good idea. Arnie is...?"

"My boyfriend."

Olivia nods and purses her lips, automatically running her hands down her designer loungewear as if getting ready for battle. "Well, all I can say is, don't look to your father and me for advice." She laughs, but it has a bitter edge even I can hear.

I'm not used to seeing my mother emotional about... anything except shopping. I don't know what to say. It's always seemed to me that Olivia Barrington (née Selznick) floated through life, not really caring about anything but who she was having lunch with on a given day. She surely never mothered Sarah-Michelle or me. But she's showing her feelings now, and it makes me wonder how much she's held back over the years… and why. Maybe she and I are more alike than I ever thought.

"You're welcome to stay here, Tobias, but things will be changing. And who knows what will happen in the next year."

I take a deep breath, because while it isn't the right time to have her meet Arnie, it feels like the right time to tell her my plans. "I'm going to be quitting Barrington. Just so you know. I was planning on it anyway. I'm going for my master's in screen-writing."

She cocks her head at me and nods again. "Good for you. I'm sure I owe you an apology for not being as supportive as I should have been over the years."

I can't help but notice that's not exactly an apology, but maybe that's a bit much to expect. I step down and move around her. "I have my phone now. Let me know if there's something you need."

I'd offer to call someone, but I have no idea who Olivia's true friends are, and I'm wondering if she knows either. I know who mine are.

Back outside, I slink around the side of the house to the front. Thankfully my father is gone—or, at least, his BMW isn't parked in the drive. I breathe a sigh of relief and jog across the street to where Arnie is waiting for me. I am so lucky.

"Hey," I call out. Arnie turns at the sound of my voice. "You're amazing, and I love you."

He flushes bright red, glancing over at my sister and Rowan, who're grinning like Cheshire cats, but I'm not sorry about telling him right then. I couldn't keep it to myself any longer.

And, after a lifetime of living in a house where nothing was said, I refuse to live that way any longer. I'm going to tell Arnie I love him all the time.

The porch door opens, and Charley shuffles out looking as disheveled as I have ever seen him. His blond hair is sticking out all over his head. He's wearing sleep pants and a tattered T-shirt that possibly once had a logo or slogan on it but is now unreadable.

"You look like crap," Arnie says cheerfully. "It's nice to know you actually are human. I think, anyway."

Charley glowers at him. To me, he says, "What's going on?"

THIRTY

Chapter Thirty—Arnie

I'M nervous about this interview, but, honestly, a significant amount of my brain space is filled with Tobias Barrington telling me he loves me. I keep finding myself drifting back to sitting on the porch with his sister and her friend, and Tobias yelling the words from across the street—in public! In front of everyone! Like he really meant them.

It took me a second to process what had happened. First, I thought he'd said, "You're amazing and I love you." Which he had, but he couldn't possibly mean me—could he? I'd glanced at Sarah-Michelle and Rowan, and they'd been grinning at me. Me? It didn't feel real. How could Tobias love *me*?

Ashley Herrmann, the HR representative interviewing me, interrupts my thoughts. "Mr. Ferguson, your resume is interesting, but tell me a little about yourself and why you're leaving"—she glances at the sheet of paper sitting on the desk in front of her—"Barrington Properties after only having been there a few weeks."

Tobias's smiling face flashes in front of my eyes again: his long eyelashes, full bottom lip, eyebrows like crows' wings. We've been officially dating six weeks, and he's become my whole world. Before Tobias, I was boring Arnie who'd been working at the same coffee shop for a couple of years, hating his life. Tobias arrived, and everything changed—for the better.

"Revenge," I say.

Ashley frowns. "Excuse me?"

Leaning back in my seat, I laugh, and my twitchy stomach settles a bit. I'm going to tell this complete stranger my tale of love and revenge.

"I was in a rut, so"—I pause to find the right words—"I decided the only way to get myself *out* of the rut was to find this guy who I'd known a long time ago and, uh, get even with him." I'm blushing. My nerves flood back, making me feel slightly queasy. I really want this job, but I've started and need to finish this. "Because, see, I was going to infiltrate his work, date him—I never really figured out in what order that would be, date first or infiltrate first—and then I'd break up with him and we'd be even. I mean, my plan never really got off the ground—except I did end up getting hired at Barrington.

"Let me be the first to tell you that the best-laid plans of this gay man—if it had been the best plan, which it wasn't—went awry. In the best possible way. Instead of getting even, I, we, actually fe—are dating now. For real. So it's probably for the best I don't stay at Barrington, given that I applied out of spite, not because I really wanted to work there."

I notice she doesn't cringe when I announce I'm gay. I want to get that out there right away in case there's a problem. A company can say it's LGBT-friendly all it wants, but HR is where it matters—or so I've been told. I also notice she's biting her lip and, perhaps, suppressing a chuckle?

"Mr. Ferguson, that's delightful. I'm wondering, though..."

She taps her lip with her index finger and asks, "Is there anyone here at our company you're considering taking down? You aren't applying here for the same reason?"

"What? No!" I stare at her in shock. "I would never!"

"But you did," she points out.

"I did, but just the one time! I'll never do it again, I swear!" I never should have said anything. Now my palms are sweaty. I reach up and try to loosen my tie and collar, which feel too tight.

Now she does laugh, and after a second I laugh too—because it was a ridiculous thing to have done.

"Tell me why you applied at Puzzle Box."

I launch into my explanation about how I think it's a cool company and I have a lot to offer. Not only am I a nerdy numbers geek, I'm also a history buff with a lot of random knowledge that would be good for research and designing online puzzles and trivia games.

An hour later I'm back out on the streets of downtown Seattle, feeling pretty good about the interview. Tobias told me to be myself, and I think, for once, it may have paid off.

My heart yearns—yes, *yearns*—for Tobias. But he's dealing with the fallout from his father's affair.

If I hadn't already known Tobias was brilliant, the Monday morning after the scene at his parents' house would've confirmed it. Tobias may not like the real estate business, but he understands how people work.

Tobias called an all-staff meeting early that morning, and by eleven the immediate operations of Barrington Properties had been reorganized. Andrew Barrington, the staff was told, was taking some time off to "deal with his personal affairs." Ha, if sifting through the carnage of his marriage is taking care of affairs. I haven't asked Tobias where his father is, but if my business were in jeopardy, I'd be doing everything I could to bolster morale and get employees to focus, not hiding.

A temp agency sent someone over to take Carly's spot at the front desk. Perry is about my age and cute as a button. Tobias had spent that Sunday night calling around to find a real estate lawyer to look over all the paperwork being prepared for closings, just to be sure everything was above board. Barrington's reputation has taken enough of a hit; they don't need any further scandal or accusations of misdeeds.

I linger in front of the Puzzle Box building for a minute, trying to decide what to do next. Fall is definitely in the air, and it's my absolute favorite season. My gaze drifts to the coffee stand outside Westlake Center, which is bustling this blustery afternoon. I decide to wander over and get a coffee before deciding what to do next. Now that I don't work at the Buzz, I don't have access to unlimited caffeine, which is something that's taking a bit of getting used to.

The same barista from when I was here with my mom, Sam, is pulling espressos. There's no reason to think he'd remember me, and I'm looking extra spiffy today in one of the suits my mom bought me that day, so I just order a doppio and move to wait at the end of the counter. A breeze blows a couple of dry leaves down the sidewalk. They tumble after each other as if they're playing a friendly game of tag.

My phone buzzes against my thigh, and I'm reaching for it as Sam sets my drink down.

Tobias: WHERE ARE YOU

Arnie: WESTLAKE COFFEE

Tobias: DON'T MOVE!

A COUPLE OF MINUTES LATER, Tobias jogs around the corner. I can tell when he spots me sitting at one of the café tables strung along the sidewalk. A broad smile breaks across his face.

"Hey," he says as he sits in the chair across from me.

"Hey back." I can't help but smile. It's like my face is in love with his face.

"How'd it go?"

"Pretty good, I think. What are you doing here? Aren't you supposed to be putting out fires at work?"

Not that I'm not incredibly happy to see him—note my face—but I don't want to get him in trouble.

"All the little fires are under control, for now. I talked to Andrew, and he'll be back next week."

"That's good?"

Tobias shrugs. "I suppose. Good for me, anyway. I gave him my notice; said I'd stay through the end of the year."

"How'd he take it?"

Tobias lifts a shoulder up and lets it back down. "About as I expected. He blustered. Huffed and puffed about family duty. I pointed out that he'd pretty much blown that out of the water. And I'm not changing my mind, so it doesn't matter what he says."

More leaves tumble past. The wind has an edge to it now, making me shiver. I sip the last of my espresso and toss my empty cup into the trash at the end of the cart. "Two points." I shake my hips like I'm some sort of sports star.

"That was pure luck."

It was, but I refuse to admit it. Same as it was pure luck Tobias thinks he's in love with me. I am too—in love with him. I'll tell him soon, but I think he already knows. He's brilliant.

THIRTY-ONE

Epilogue—Arnie

I'M NOT GOING to cry. I'm not going to cry... I silently repeat the words to myself over and over as the couple stands together in front of their wedding guests. My mom is vibrant in a gray-blue lace gown that reaches to her calves and makes her long auburn hair pop. The groom doesn't look too bad himself, in a steel-blue tuxedo a shade or two lighter than Mom's dress.

They chose not to have attendants, something for which I am eternally grateful. Rita and Will walked together down the aisle. When I asked my mom who was giving her away, I ended up on the receiving end of a lecture about outdated mores, caveman-like behavior, and how she could make it fifty feet on her own, thank you very much.

Okay, then, no giving away. She wasn't mine to keep anyway, which I guess is one of the things I've learned over the past months. Surreptitiously I lift a hand to swipe at the moisture on my cheek. Not crying.

Leaning into me, Tobias whispers, "It's okay if you cry. It's a wedding. I think you're kind of supposed to."

The past few months have been a whirlwind of wedding planning, getting started at my new job, and wanting to spend all the time I can with Tobias.

Whether despite or because of my unorthodox interview, I'm now happily employed by a local company that designs online games. They create virtual breakout puzzle rooms, and I do research for the games as well as other projects. It's fun, and for the first time I'm really using my Latin degree—who knew?

Tobias squeezes my hand, and the audience quiets as soft music starts to play. A friend of Will's was ordained by the Universal Life Church. The cheat sheet for their vows shakes in his grip.

"Dearly beloved..." he begins.

By the end of the ceremony, I'm a mess. Luckily, Tobias has a seemingly endless supply of tissues, making me wonder about the depth of his pockets. By the time it's our turn to greet the newly married couple, I manage to appear composed.

Olivia and Sarah-Michelle Barrington were invited too and are standing on the other side of Tobias. When my mom found out about Tobias's parents, she reached out to Olivia, and they've become friends. I'm pretty sure Olivia doesn't really know what hit her. Tobias was a bit confused at first too, but I think it's given him a chance to see Olivia in another light—without his dad around. My mom has always adopted the strays—Duff, for instance—and before they know it, boom, they're family.

Speaking of Duff, he's standing on my other side, with Will's daughters on the other side of him. As I glance over at him, he's tucking a tissue into his suitcoat pocket. Catching my eye, he gifts me with a half smile. Now that Tobias and I are sorted out and the wedding is over, I need to figure out what the heck is going on with my best friend. My work is never done.

A FEW HOURS LATER, the reception begins to wind down. Mom finds me where I'm sitting with Tobias, trying to catch my breath from being spun around on the dance floor. We took swing dance lessons this past fall, but all I've learned is that I have two left feet. Tobias is, of course, a beautiful dancer who doesn't mind that I step on his toes occasionally.

He also dances with both of my new stepsisters, saving their toes from me.

"We're leaving, honey," Mom says, her smile bright but a little tired at the edges.

"Okay."

Tobias and I follow her to where Will waits with Alex and Jo and a few other people near the front entrance. A town car is idling at the curb, ready to whisk them to the airport for their honeymoon. Mom kisses me on the cheek and continues walking, ending up next to her husband, grabbing his hand as if it's a lifeline. It's adorable. I sigh. I am so happy for my mom, and Will too. He can stay. He's the perfect addition to our family. I mean, I know it wasn't my choice, but I do like him.

I'm a bit distracted. The ceremony, dancing, and delicious food and wine have me in a bit of a daze. Something flies toward me, and without thinking, I raise my hands to keep it from beaning me—and accidentally catch it. Everyone starts clapping, and it takes me a moment to realize I'm holding Mom's bouquet.

"Oh, god, how did that happen?" I ask the bouquet.

My mom smiles even more broadly, waving as she turns to the door. Will wraps his coat around her, and they head out into the cold Seattle weather. Will bundles her into the town car, and too soon they are gone, heading to Sea-Tac and Hawaii.

I don't know what to do with the bouquet. The beautiful arrangement of lilies, mums, and twisted willow feels like a hot potato in my hands. Turning, I try to hand it off to someone, anyone—it wasn't meant for me—but the rest of the goodbye group has started to drift away to retrieve their own coats and bags from the concierge and head home.

Tobias wraps his arm around my shoulders and whispers into my ear, "Not tomorrow or anything, but soon, if you'll have me, we'll be having a ceremony of our own."

"What?" I squeak as my entire body freezes—or melts, I'm not sure which.

"I want to get married, Arnie Ferguson. To you."

"But," I sputter, because yes, I do too, but I still have a hard time believing Tobias wants to be with me. Forever.

"You're the only one I want, Arnie. I mean, we waited years until we found each other again. I don't actually think we're hurrying anything."

God damn it, I start to cry again. "Yes," I manage, "I want to get married too. To you. I love you, Tobias Barrington."

EPILOGUE

Epilogue—Tobias

"COME ON," I implore. I'm as excited as a six-year-old going to a birthday party, but Arnie is immovable. He's curled up on his futon with a book and obviously has no plans to leave the apartment building anytime soon.

"I only have, like, five pages left."

"You said that a half hour ago."

"Yeah, and if you'd quit pestering me, I'd be finished by now."

I sigh loudly. Then I put on my coat and start shaking my keys. I've been staying with Arnie when Duff travels for photo shoots, which is often. Or when he's staying with "a friend," a phrase that makes Arnie roll his eyes so hard I'm afraid they'll stick that way.

Arnie puts his e-reader down, shaking his head regretfully before asking, "What is so important that I have to leave the house?"

The winter weather has arrived with an evil swagger. It's

been cloudy and rainy in Seattle for weeks. Most of the population has hunkered down for the duration, although there is a significant percentage who ignore the weather and continue to wear shorts and sandals and ride their bikes as if Mother Nature weren't actively trying to drown them. I am not one of those people, but today I have something I want to show Arnie... and he's being stubborn.

"Just this one time, can we go without twenty-one questions?"

"Twenty questions."

"What are you talking about?"

"It's twenty questions, so sure, we'll go after twenty."

I sigh again. "For crying out loud."

His lips part slightly, and he bites the tip of his tongue. I realize then he's purposely giving me a hard time. His auburn hair is standing on end, his glasses are ever-so-slightly askew, and he's let his beard grow in just a little. I cannot resist this man.

My feet carry me to his side; he's magnetic, and I'm iron. "How long have you been done with your book?" I demand.

He leans back against the futon, his hazel eyes filled with mirth. "I swear, I just finished it!"

This is a patent lie, of this I am sure. Kneeling on the edge of the cushion, I take his face between my hands, loving the scratchy feel of his beard underneath my fingers. There are so many things to love about him. His expression transforms from humor to want, and he licks his lips. Even though I want to get going, I can't help myself: I lean in and press my lips against his.

Kissing Arnie has quickly become one of my favorite things in the world. Groaning, I push him down into the cushion. His erection presses against mine in spite of the denim between us, and I grind against him, licking into his open mouth and sucking on his lower lip. He's arching up against me, and suddenly I'm desperate and the reason I wanted to leave can wait a few more minutes. This is not going to take long.

Arnie shoves my sweatshirt up and begins sucking on my nipples. I had no idea I was a nipple man before Arnie. "Jesus Christ," I pant.

Jamming a hand between us, I unfasten my jeans and free my cock—thank god for going commando—before I pull down his sweatpants so I can reach his hot, hard erection. Rain is smacking against the window, and a sneaky draft that has made its way through a weak spot in the windowsill is caressing my bare back. It's not cooling me down. Arnie lures my tongue into his mouth. He's sucking on it like it's my dick, and one of us groans with pleasure. As I pump us together, both slick and wet in my grasp, the familiar electric feeling pools at the base of my spine. Arnie keeps my tongue captive and pinches a nipple, and the pleasure-pain of it sends me over the edge.

"Oh, god, Arnie." I pump desperately against his body, reveling in the pressure and the friction. I've reached liftoff; hot liquid spills over my knuckles as we come together, Arnie shouting "Fuck!" as he grinds his hips upward.

For a minute I lie on top of him, panting as I regain my breath.

"I love you, Tobias."

My favorite words in the world.

"I love you too, Arnie."

He blushes a little, or maybe his color is from having a massive orgasm. Either way, I love it.

"WHY ARE WE HERE?"

Here is across the street from Barrington Properties, but that's not where we're headed. Arnie hates surprises. I'm hoping he forgives me for this one; it's a biggie.

"Come on, already."

Grumbling about the weather and Saturdays being for reading and sex, he follows me. We pass the building, and he glances at me quizzically.

"Just a little farther, I swear."

I lead the way to the walking path along Lake Union, and we follow it for about a block before I turn onto a smaller, gated path—one to which I have the code.

"This is private property," Arnie says.

"It is," I reply.

"Okaaay."

Chuckling, I grab his hand and drag him through the gate. Together we walk down the ramp to the dock where a number of floating homes are moored: four on each side, with a few others moored off side piers.

Floating homes are like people, even more than houses built on land. They are eclectic, colorful, and eccentric. Every home on this dock is different. A few of them are no more than five hundred square feet; one on the end is much larger and three stories tall.

Across from the huge house floats a medium-sized one-and-a-half-story home. It has a nice kitchen open to the large living room that looks out over the lake. There's a deck, and a bathroom with both a shower and a tub—rare for a floating home. The half story is the bedroom, which has skylights and a slider that opens to another deck just large enough for two loungers and a small umbrella. The bed is custom-built to fit in the room, and there is a ton of built-in storage. I know this because I've been in negotiations to purchase this home, but I didn't want to say anything until I knew it was happening.

Arnie thinks he needs to have a better job before we get a place together. He's still pretty new at Puzzle Box.

But I don't want to wait any longer. I want to wake up with

him in the morning and go to sleep with him at night—and I can make that happen, so I did. Now I'm just hoping he isn't mad about it.

"Tobias?" Arnie asks from behind me.

Instead of looking at him, I shakily fit the key into the lock, open the front door, and step over the threshold. Only then do I turn. His eyes are wide. I can see the specks of gold that float in them.

"Welcome home?" I say. Unfortunately, the words come out a bit like a question.

Arnie's lips part, but he doesn't say anything. Dazed, he follows me into our new house. His eyes dart everywhere, trying to take in everything at once as we stand in the tiny foyer with the tiny staircase off to the left.

"Let me show you the best part—"

"Oh, no you don't!" Arnie grabs my hand before I can mount the stairs. "You show me the whole thing first, and save the best part for last. But Tobias, I don't know what to say. I can never pay you back. This is much, much more than I can afford."

I kiss him, to make him be quiet.

When we come up for air, I say, "Arnie, I want you. I don't care about money—and before you can argue, I put you on the deed. When I'm in school or trying to sell screenplays, you'll be the one taking care of me. Let me do this."

We spend an hour checking out the main level. Arnie literally leaves no door drawer unopened. From the living room we can see Gas Works Park and beyond to the locks. Even though it's still pissing down rain, we stand out on the lower deck for ages, our arms around each other's waists.

A lone kayaker floats by, his bright orange vessel vibrant against the gray. "I'm not doing *that*," Arnie whispers in my ear.

"Mmm," is all I say in reply. Arnie likes to say stuff like that.

I like convincing him otherwise. I bet myself a dollar I can get him out on a kayak when summer returns.

Finally, I drag him upstairs to the bedroom. When Arnie gets his first glimpse, he gasps and I grin.

"I did okay?"

In addition to the built-in bed, custom bookshelves are built across from it. We'll have room for all the books he could ever want. We can lie in bed and watch the world through the doors to the deck. I imagine us having sex up here—I have a very active imagination.

Arnie's gaze catches my own, and I know he's thinking the same thing.

"We can't," I say. Well, we could, but there are no sheets and no window shades yet.

"Fine." He turns back to look out at our view again.

Crossing the room to stand behind him, I wrap my arms around him and tug him tight. I love his body against mine, any way I can get it. Arnie is... flighty and funny. He sees the world through a slightly off-center prism. He doesn't like change; he'll fight it every step of the way. He is also stubborn and independent. When he gets an idea in his head... let's just say I like distracting him with blow jobs.

I knew I'd never be able to convince him to even tour the house, so I took out a bridge loan on my trust and everything is taken care of. This home is one of a kind, and I can't wait to live here with him. Now we have a forever home.

"Do you forgive me?" I ask, pulling him even closer.

He grumbles but leans back, letting me take his weight. "This time."

I crook my head and press my face against his neck. I don't bother to hide my smile, and I know he can see it in the reflection from the sliding glass door. Arnie thinks he doesn't bring enough to our relationship, that he's a drag. I guess I'm going to spend a lifetime convincing him otherwise.

Arnie is just what I need. He makes me smile, he's smart as a whip, and he has the heart of a lion. I can't imagine loving anyone else the way I love him. Who knew, when I impulsively stopped for a coffee all those months ago, I would find the man of my dreams behind the counter?

"I love you, Tobias. I can't believe you did this. Well, I can, but... I love you."

There's a funny hitch to his voice. Leaning back, I turn him around so I can see his face. There are tears in his eyes.

He looks up at me, hazel eyes wide behind his glasses. "I never thought, never believed... that you could love me."

"Believe it," I say as I lower my lips to his to demonstrate exactly how much I in fact love Arnie Ferguson.

CURIOUS ABOUT DUFF'S BACKSTORY? Join my newsletter so you can read Heart-Loss for FREE before diving into The Heart Heist.

Still not ready to leave the Seattle boys? How about a teaser for The Boyfriend Spree? Night at the Museum is a short free read for my newsletter subscribers.

THE HEART HEIST is Duff and Jacob's story, read it today. Followed by **The Boyfriend Gambit**.

IF YOU ENJOY SWEET, low-angst, high-heat mm romance, check out the Home in Hollyridge novella series beginning with Love Limited Edition.

Will bookish magic, an adorable dog, and a little assistance from their friends, help Brett and Rory realize the world is what you make of it, that a chance at happiness is something to be seized, not tossed aside?

CHECK out the first in my Veiled Intentions romantic suspense series, **Conspiracy Theory**. A jaded big city detective and a small town Sheriff meet again...murder brings Niall and Mat together, will it tear them apart?

"There is a dog. The dog does not die. There's a dramatic backstory, there's murder, and there are strong wonderful characters to warm toe heart." *5-stars for Conspiracy Theory (reviewer)*

If you enjoyed Feinted Love, I would greatly appreciate if you would let your friends know so they can experience Arnie, Tobias and the rest of the gang. As with all of my books, I have enabled lending on all platforms in which it is allowed to make it easy to share with a friend. If you leave a review for *Feinted Love,* or any of my books. on the site from which you purchased the book, Goodreads, Bookbub or your own blog, I would love to read it! Email me the link at elle@ellekeaton.com

Keep up-to-date with new releases and sales, *The Highway to Elle* hits your in-box approximately every two weeks, sometimes more sometimes less. I include deals, freebies and new releases as well as a sort of rambling running commentary on what *this* author's life is like. I'd love to have you aboard! I also have a reader group called the Highway to Elle, come say hi!

ABOUT ELLE

Elle hails from the northwest corner of the US known for, rain, rain, and more rain. She pens the Shielded Hearts, Veiled Intentions, West Coast Forensics, Home in Hollyridge and Crimes of the Heart series' all set in the Pacific Northwest. Elle is chief cook and bottle washer, the one always asking 'where are my keys and/or wallet' and 'why are there cats?' (This question not yet answered).

Elle *loves* both cats and dogs, Star Wars and Star Trek, pineapple on pizza, and is known to start crossword puzzles with ballpoint pen.

Thank you for supporting this Indie Author,

Elle

Thank you, to a dedicated group of beta readers and fellow author critiques who worked above and beyond to help me shape Arnie and Tobias's story into Feinted Love, I couldn't have done it without you. Books are not created in a vacuum and every single person I consulted helped me beyond measure.

Thank you to MrE who supports me every step of the way, I couldn't do anything without you. I am the lucky one, so there.

I truly hope you enjoy Feinted Love and Arnie and Tobias, I'm fairly sure most of us remember the awkwardness of falling in love for the first time.

The City of Seattle deserves a thank you as well. The entire Crimes of the Heart series is set in my hometown, I hope readers learn something about it aside from the Space Needle and that it rains a lot. While it has changed in recent years (heck, in recent months) Broadway has always been the epicenter of queer culture in Seattle; one of the safer places to hold hands and be yourself. It's also incredibly culturally diverse, a place worth visiting if you come to our fair city. Madison, Leschi, Madrona, Greenwood, the U-District, Lake Union, are just a few of the neighborhoods in Seattle. Garlic Gulch is a real place, although it's now called Columbia City.

Thank you again for taking a chance on Feinted Love,

Elle Keaton

ACKNOWLEDGMENTS

There are many to be made…thank you;

I used many real businesses in Seattle; Tougo Coffee, The De Luxe, Dick's Drive-In, The Egyptian Theater, Bartell Drugs, P.F. Chang's, The Seattle Kraken. Thank you for existing!

(The Buzz exists only in my imagination, the Blue is loosely modeled after the Blue Water in Leschi. The Taste of the Andes is also a product of my imagination.)

Thank you to the following artists for their inspiration:

Lady Gaga for "Born This Way".

Soft Cell for "Tainted Love".

Green Day for "American Idiot".

The old 97s

Daft Punk for "Get Lucky".

America for "A Horse with No Name".

Yusuf Islam, in general, for keeping me writing.

The following movies are mentioned in passing:

Down by Law; written and directed by Jim Jarmusch.

Leaving Las Vegas (1995); based on the book by Jim O'Brien written and directed by Mike Figgis

Little Miss Sunshine (2006); Screenplay by Michael Arndt, directed by Jonathan Dayton and Valerie Faros.

Napoleon Dynamite (2004); written by Jared and Jerusha Hess, directed by Jared Hess. Produced by Jeremy Coon, Chris Wyatt, Sean Covel and Jory Weitz.

Ocean's Eleven (2001); directed by Steven Soderbergh and written by Ted Griffin.

Repo Man (1984); written and directed by Alex Cox

Risky Business (1983); written and directed by Paul Brickman.

Vegas Vacation (1997); Directed by Stephen Kessler, written by Elisa Bell, based on a story by Bell and Bob Ducsay.